"Hello."

Her voice was as soft as she looked, and as inviting. It took Ken a split second to realize he hadn't answered her.

"Hello. Are you a wedding guest?"

Janet hesitated a moment. "Sort of. Are you?"

He grinned. "Sort of."

They stood for a moment, examining each other. Against his better judgment, Ken threw caution to the wind. What he was about to do was crazy. But his emotions were involved, and impulse overruled common sense.

"Please don't take this the wrong way, but you are a truly beautiful woman. Would you do me the honor of having dinner with me some evening?"

Janet's smile froze as she acknowledged silently how very much she would *love* to have dinner with him some evening. But in less than an hour she would be Mrs. Kenneth Radnor, and despite the fact that she had never met him she was obligated to play the part of his devoted wife. It was time to tell the man before her who she was before they were both embarrassed. But when the stranger took her hand, it made speaking all the more difficult.

Suddenly Edmund Radnor opened the door and saw his brother, Kenneth, holding the hand of his future wife.

"Well! I see you've both met. That saves me the trouble of awkward introductions!"

Dear Reader:

So many of you asked for him, and now you've got him: Shiloh Butler, Mr. November. *Shiloh's Promise* by BJ James, is the long-awaited sequel to *Twice in a Lifetime*. Not only do many of your favorite characters reappear, but the enigmatic and compelling Shiloh now has his very own story—and his own woman!

And coming in December... *Wilderness Child* by Ann Major. This tie-in to her *Children of Destiny* series winds up 1989 in a very exciting way....

I've been telling you so much about the *Man of the Month* program that I want to mention some other exciting plans we have in store for you. Celeste Hamilton will be starting a trilogy in December with *The Diamond's Sparkle*. And the next few months will be bringing you Desires from such favorites as Katherine Granger, Linda Lael Miller and Dixie Browning....

So go wild with Desire—you'll be glad you did!

All the best,

Lucia Macro
Senior Editor

AUDRA ADAMS

BLUE CHIP BRIDE

SILHOUETTE *Desire*

Published by Silhouette Books New York

America's Publisher of Contemporary Romance

SILHOUETTE BOOKS
300 East 42nd St., New York, N.Y. 10017

ISBN: 0-373-05532-3

First Silhouette Books printing November 1989

Printed in the U.S.A.

AUDRA ADAMS

has always been in love with love, and happy endings are a prerequisite for a love story. What better reason to become a romance writer? She has stored away a wellspring of inspiration, from her first readings of "Cinderella" right up to meeting her husband, who proposed eight days after they met. "They" said it wouldn't last, but eleven years and two children later the marriage is still going strong.

Audra Adams is a transplanted New York City woman who has fallen under the spell of the Jersey shore, dreaming up new characters and stories as she stares for hours out at the rolling ocean waves. She's an incurable optimist who feels that life should be lived to the fullest and, if it is, romance will find you.

To Helen Cavanagh—
teacher, mentor, friend,
She dared to dream it . . .
and . . .
To Jim,
for his love, support
and, most of all,
the luxury of time.

Prologue

—————

What are you trying to tell me, Paul?"

She was stalling. She knew *exactly* what her lawyer was trying to say in the nicest way possible. She, Janet Demarest, recent widow of business tycoon Jonathan Demarest, was broke. Flat out, bottom line broke.

"Don't coddle me. If I'm going to be able to take care of Peter, I need to know the truth."

She watched as he sighed. In that instant she realized this was a long time coming. J.D. had been Paul's colleague, his mentor, his friend, but they had vehemently disagreed on many business practices. Especially in the past few years. Especially since the accident.

J.D. had not only lost his first wife in a horrible car crash ten years ago, but he'd been crippled, as well. He'd been left with useless legs and a six-year-old son who was bewildered and afraid of his bitter, paralyzed father. J.D.'s sister, Katherine, had brought in a young au pair girl to care for Peter. Janet remembered that at eighteen she'd felt as lost and as longing for affection as the small, lonely boy. Together they'd formed a strong, loving relationship.

A few eyebrows had raised at the time of Janet and J.D.'s May-December wedding. Janet knew everyone had wondered what kind of marriage it would be. J.D. had been incapable of any physical relationship, but no one knew that to be fact, so speculation had run rampant. She'd good-naturedly allowed the sometimes off-color remarks of J.D.'s cronies over the years. They were harmless and in a way made J.D. feel good about himself. For who were those people to judge? Janet had blossomed under J.D.'s tutelage, developing poise and grace as well as fulfilling the promise of her womanly beauty. He'd sent her to college, making her career as a counselor at the university possible, a job she loved and was well suited for. She'd been his wife for eight years, and now she was his widow.

She observed Paul's turmoil, but needed to be told the truth in no uncertain terms.

"Please, Paul."

Paul Bradly expelled a long breath before sitting on the sofa. "Okay, Janet, you win. To put it bluntly and without a lot of legalese, there's no money left, or at best, very little. Certainly not enough to maintain this life-style." He waved his arm at the elegantly furnished room.

"This isn't possible, Paul! What about all the various companies J.D. controlled?"

"I'm afraid somewhere along the line his partners outmaneuvered him. Over the years, he'd taken out loans with his stock as collateral, and he never paid them off. The stock reverted to the other partners. J.D. died owning no part of J.D. Enterprises."

"But this house—"

"Mortgaged."

"None of this makes sense. J.D. was a shrewd businessman. He worked every day of our married life. His will gave no indication of financial trouble. How could he leave me all his businesses and stocks and this house if he didn't own any of them?" Her voice rose gradually as she spoke, and she felt the beginnings of hysteria.

"Janet, please, calm down. Sit and have some coffee, and I'll explain as best I can."

She stared at him for a moment before complying.

"First of all," he began, "when J.D. wrote that will at the beginning of your marriage, he still *did* own everything." Paul stood up abruptly and paced the room. "I wish you'd known J.D. before. Before the accident, that is. He was sharp as a tack! But sitting in a wheelchair day after day changed him. Everyone said he'd snapped back, and he had, or so it seemed on the surface. But underneath—" he tapped his chest "—in here, something was gone. Life became a game. And so did business. He became involved in schemes, fly-by-night deals. He lost money, lots of it. And what he didn't lose he spent. He didn't care, Janet. When I would speak to him about it, he would laugh, tell me I was getting old. After several arguments, I gave up. What was I to do? It was his money, after all."

"Go on," she said, her expression as cold as stone.

"Well, things got out of hand. First he lost the companies, then the stocks. He mortgaged this house to the hilt. Then he tried to break into Peter's trust and had some success—"

"No! Not Peter's money, too!"

"Not all of it. Toward the end, J.D. was able to prove to the court that he needed the money for Peter's education, and because it was for the child's welfare, they allowed him access to some of the trust fund. Peter still has a decent nest egg—'' Paul stopped pacing and stood over her ''—but I'm sorry to say that J.D.'s legacy is mostly all gone.''

"This is incredible."

"I know it's a shock, Janet. I told J.D. many times to confide in you, but he always felt he'd make the money back. He didn't expect to die."

They stared at each other for a moment in silence, sharing the sorrow of their mutual loss. Janet stood and walked to the French doors. The late-summer sun was barely touching the tops of the trees in the artistically landscaped backyard. She pictured Peter playing on the lawn, as was common during his vacation. Their home was an old-fashioned colonial nestled on two acres of land in the Westchester community of Rye, New York. It was an area of wealth and privilege, and Peter had been born in it. The last conversation they'd had was in this yard, after the funeral. Peter had asked her if he would have to leave his private boarding school now that his father was dead. Hugging him tightly, she'd assured him that nothing would change, nothing....

"What am I going to do, Paul?" Janet asked, still staring out beyond the trees. "I don't care about myself. I have my job at the university. It doesn't pay much, but I can certainly live well enough. But Peter?" She paused and shook her head. "He's never been poor. He doesn't know the first thing about it. I've already promised him he wouldn't have to leave school. Carlton is so expensive! Oh, God, he's had so many tragedies in his life already—why this, why now?"

Janet buried her face in her hands, then took a breath, deep in thought.

"Well," she continued, "I suppose the first thing to do is sell the house and dismiss the servants."

"Perhaps Katherine will help."

Janet laughed and slowly shook her head. "Katherine is very good with charity cases, as you and I well know. I wouldn't be here today if she hadn't taken me from that foster home. But she goes only so far. She doesn't get too close, too involved. I'll have to find another way." She walked toward the portable bar in the corner of the room and poured each of them a drink.

"You're a remarkable woman, Janet," Paul said. "I must admit you're taking this a lot better than I thought."

"Thought I'd crumble?" She smiled as he nodded. "I am crumbling. Inside. I'm just too scared or too stupid to realize it yet!"

"You're neither. I think you're brave, and very, very strong."

"Thank you, Paul. It's not true, but thank you."

Janet handed him his drink and took a long sip of hers as she walked toward the window and watched the sun dip lower. They'd been talking all afternoon.

"There *may* be one solution."

She turned to look at him.

"I didn't bring it up earlier, because, frankly, I didn't think you'd consider it. But you're taking this so well, you might want to think about it."

"For heaven's sake, Paul, stop being so cryptic! What are you talking about?"

"Have you ever heard of Radnor Corporation?"

"No."

"Well, the family's from town. They own a fairly large corporation—"

"What does this have to do with me?"

"You own fifteen percent of it—well, J.D. did, anyway. He and Gil Radnor were friends way back when, and as a young man J.D. worked for him. At that time, the company was small and there weren't any profits to speak of, so Radnor paid J.D. with stock. Before he left to go out on his own, he'd accumulated fifteen percent. It wasn't worth much then, but now it's a tidy sum."

"Why wasn't this stock lost, also?"

"Because J.D. couldn't borrow against it. Old Gil Radnor was smart. He made J.D. a partner, but on the condition that if he ever wanted to use the stock in any way or sell it, he'd have to approach the Radnor family first, giving them a year to exercise the option. J.D. didn't want to do that for reasons of personal pride, so he kept the stock intact. Gil always wanted to keep all corporate stock in the family, and his sons have carried on the tradition."

"That's wonderful! Let's sell it back to them now."

"I've checked it out already with Edmund—he's the eldest son and president—and yes, in a way, you can, but it's a little more complicated than an out-and-out sale."

"Why?"

"Currently the Radnors are involved in a new project and are short of capital—it's all reinvested in a newly acquired company with no short-term return. They need time—"

"But I can't wait. Can't we tell them I need the money now?"

"I already have. I also told him that your primary concern was Peter. I figured at this point there was no need to pull any punches, and he suggested a solution, so to speak."

"And..." Janet waved her hands for him to continue.

"And I turned him down."

"Why? What was the solution? Lord, Paul, right now I can't think of anything I wouldn't do to get my hands on some money!"

"To be perfectly honest, I said no because I didn't think you'd go for it. Hell, *I* didn't go for it!"

"Paul, for heaven's sake, what did the man suggest?"

"He suggested you marry his brother."

One

Kenneth Gilbert Radnor ran his hand indecisively through the built-in tie rack in his closet. Pulling out a silk navy-and-white striped tie, he held it up to his floor-length mirrored image. Satisfied, he wrapped the tie around the collar of his new white shirt and walked toward the window.

His apartment was located in the east wing of the Radnor house, on the third floor. The rooms were decidedly masculine in decor and still held some of the traces of the boy he once had been. Ken kept a town house in New York City, but when all was said and done, this was home and these rooms his sanctuary. He shared the enormous house with his elder brother, Edmund, and his family, who occupied the entire second floor. Brian, his younger brother, had a similar apartment in the west wing, but it was possible for weeks to go by before they would even bump into each other. The management of the house ran smoothly, however, due to the diligent eyes of Edmund's wife, Eleanor.

Ken tugged on both ends of the tie in frustration as he watched the cars pull into the circular driveway. Guests arriving for the wedding. *Wedding*. Farce, would be more like it! What was supposed to have been a simple, private ceremony in front of a justice of the peace had snowballed into a lavishly catered affair once Eleanor had become involved. The brothers had agreed not to tell Eleanor the true nature of this marriage. An incurable romantic, she would have been appalled at the idea of such an arrangement and none of them wanted to be subjected to what was sure to be limitless lectures on the matter.

But one would have thought Edmund would have more control over his own wife! The intended short ceremony had suddenly taken on circus proportions, complete with an audience of two hundred relatives and friends salivating in anticipation of seeing him walk down the aisle once again.

No one thought Ken Radnor would ever marry again, least of all himself. It had been almost ten years since his first wife had left him, but the thought still rankled. Not that he still carried a torch for the woman. Ken had stopped loving her approximately seventy-two hours after the wedding, when it sank in what a barracuda she was. He'd finally lost her, after eighteen months of marriage, to someone else—someone older, smarter and undoubtedly more wealthy. His male pride had been stung and the resentment ran deep. There were women in his life after that, but none could coax a commitment out of him.

Until now. Damn Edmund! His brother had inherited their father's autocratic personality. He was only six years older than Ken, but it might as well have been a generation, as Edmund always treated him as a recalcitrant child.

Ken remembered the night his brother had hit him with this absurd proposal. He'd just returned from a very long business trip, when Edmund had called him into the study to discuss a serious matter. It seemed that Jonathan Demarest had died broke, leaving his fifteen percent of the company stock up in the air, or, to be more precise, in the hands of his widow. It had always been the family's goal to return the stock to the fold, but to Ken's mind that had meant buying it back, not marrying it.

But they couldn't buy it back at the moment, not with the huge reinvestment in equipment they'd just made. And the lady needed the money now to support her stepson. Why marriage? Ken had asked. Why not just support her for a year or so?

Then Edmund had said the magic word—Carmichael. Douglas Carmichael was Ken's personal nemesis, a worthy rival who'd outsmarted the Radnors at various times over the years. Doug had made no secret of the fact that he wanted a seat on the Radnor board of directors. At times Ken had wondered how far Doug would go to fulfill his dream. After his father's death five years earlier, he found out. As far as Ken was concerned, Doug was ruthless and without conscience. He considered himself a tolerant man, but in the case of Douglas Carmichael, he gave no quarter.

With J.D.'s death, Doug had a golden opportunity to achieve his goal. It was only a matter of time before the trade discovered J.D.'s legacy, and Doug would be all over the poor old widow with a lucrative cash offer. Radnor Corporation would be hard-pressed to match it, which would leave Doug with a clear field. Ken remembered the bitter taste the thought had left in his mouth.

So Edmund had proposed this marriage. He'd even gone so far as to draw up a contract stipulating that the marriage would last one year or less, depending on how quickly they could liquify their assets and pay her off. It would be a cut-and-dry business deal. The woman could support herself and her stepson, and they would be secure in the knowledge that all one hundred percent of the Radnor stock was in the family. Afterward they could annul the marriage, with no one the worse for wear.

When Ken had suggested giving Brian the job, Edmund had only laughed. Brian was young, headstrong and irresponsible. His reputation with women was renowned. Ken had to agree that Brian wasn't the person for the job.

But was *he*? Ken moved away from the window and finished dressing. He was tired—exhausted—and it wasn't even noon yet. He'd been on the road for more than three weeks straight, selling their new concept to a half-dozen companies along the way. Usually the traveling exhilarated him, but this time, he was bone weary. At thirty-six, he was ready for something more out of life than building the family business. It was time to turn the reins over to Brian. As it was, Ken had left his younger brother out in California to finish negotiating a very important contract. He'd planned to return right after the ceremony to help complete the deal, but that was impossible now. Between the ceremony and reception, the day would be gone. He would just have to leave first thing in the morning, and hope that Brian could handle the details. He grinned to himself. Nothing wrong with a baptism by fire. By the end of this trip, they would pretty well know if Brian would be able to take over the national business on his own.

Checking his appearance once again, he was satisfied with what he saw. The navy pin-striped suit was perfectly tailored to his six-feet-two-inch frame. He brushed his black hair back from his forehead, but a stubborn strand fell forward as soon as he'd finished. He looked nothing like his brothers. They were shorter, fairer and sturdier, favoring their father. Ken took after his mother's family and his dark coloring had always stuck out like a sore thumb. The difference had bothered him when he was younger as he'd vied for his father's attention, but later, as a man, he'd realized the advantage of being different.

Ken left his rooms and descended the stairs. Almost immediately his sister-in-law, Eleanor, found him and, smiling broadly, pinned a sprig of baby's breath on the lapel of his three-piece suit.

"You look dashing!"

He smiled. "I'm glad one of us is having a good time."

"Now, Kenneth, dear, is that any attitude to have on your wedding day? Behave. You're just having a bad case of cold feet."

"Temporary insanity would be a better diagnosis," he mumbled as he surveyed the foyer, nodding politely at the guests as they milled about.

"What did you say, dear?" Eleanor asked.

He turned his attention back to her. "Nothing. Where is the blushing bride, by the way?"

"What a thing to say! Kenneth, I don't know what's going on here, but my instincts tell me all is not what it appears to be."

He smiled down at the frowning woman and forced himself to reassure her. "Nonsense, Eleanor, everything is fine, but *is* she here yet?"

"Well, no. At least I don't think so. Edmund was picking her up, but I haven't seen him return. Why don't you mingle. I'm sure they'll be here soon."

Mingling was the last thing he wanted to do. What he truly wanted to was slip out the back door. Ken had a vague memory of some malicious talk at the time of J.D.'s remarriage, but since he'd never paid much attention to gossip, the specifics eluded him. Now he wished that he had. J.D. seldom socialized after his accident, and it had been ages since their paths crossed. Ken had no knowledge of the woman J.D. had married. The only thing he did know was that J.D. was pushing sixty; logic suggested that his wife must be close in age.

Ken had no desire whatsoever to marry anyone, and especially not some woman who was probably old enough to be his mother. He imagined himself helping the poor dear down the aisle while friends and family smirked. He absolutely positively was going to kill Edmund when he got his hands on him!

He needed a drink. The bar, set up in the corner of the parlor, had a line of people three deep. He sighed. The Fates were conspiring against him today. Maybe there was something stashed in the study. He made his way across the hall.

Janet stood behind the oak desk, staring out the huge bay window in the Radnor study. Her white-knuckled, clasped hands were the only outward sign of her inner turmoil.

On this bright early-autumn day, she was dressed in a long-sleeved, cream-colored silk dress with a sheer lace tunic and matching wide-brimmed hat that complemented her honey-blond hair to perfection. The very simplicity of the outfit accentuated her subtle beauty. She appeared taller in her very high heels, and the cut of the dress hugged her hips before flaring out into handkerchief points of lace below her knees. The heart-shaped, illusion neckline delicately exposed an enticing amount of cleavage. Her small waist only accentuated her curves.

Today, she knew, she looked younger than her twenty-six years, too young to be getting married for even the first time, let alone the second. But, unbelievable as it seemed, that was the reason she was here—to be married to a man she'd never met.

When Paul Bradly had initially explained this insane proposition to her, she'd laughed in his face. It was too ridiculous even to imagine. Arranged marriages happened in the nineteenth century, not in this day and age. He'd told her to think about it, and think she had, long and hard. She'd even called Katherine, J.D.'s sister, to ask her opinion. Katherine had been all for it! "Go ahead," she'd said. "It will solve all your problems!"

But what about the problems this marriage would create? It still made no sense to her. Pieces of the puzzle were missing, and no one seemed able to give her a rational explanation. Why couldn't the Radnors simply support Peter and her for the year, *then* buy her out? Because they didn't trust her, Paul had said, or anyone for that matter, where Radnor stock was concerned. They assumed she would double-cross them and sell to a competitor for the best price. Wonderful! she thought. Here she was to live in a houseful of people who thought she was greedy and self-indulgent!

But that wasn't the worst part. Peter was. The once-loving boy, whose welfare she'd been considering all along was now estranged from her. Just thinking about it nearly brought her to tears. Janet had driven up to Carlton with Paul the day after she'd formally agreed to the terms of the Radnor contract. She'd needed Paul's moral support in facing Peter with the news of her impending marriage.

After giving the matter countless hours of thought throughout many sleepless nights, Janet had decided it would be best not to tell Peter the truth about the marriage or their dire financial situation. Paul had argued that the youth was old enough and had a right to know what was going on. But while she acknowledged those facts, she felt deep down that Peter was too emotionally fragile right now. She'd observed the signs, the same symptoms of depression he'd experienced as a young boy. She wouldn't allow this additional burden to be placed on his shoulders at this time. Too many familiar things had already been taken away from him. She wouldn't allow him to nobly leave Carlton, either. He was too dear and all she had left of J.D. She had to make good on her promise to his father that she would take care of his boy. In a few months, when this was over and she had the money to keep him in the style to which he was accustomed, she would tell him the truth.

She'd been convinced she was doing the right thing, but when they'd told Peter about the marriage, his answer hadn't been just the bewilderment she'd expected, but stone-cold scorn she hadn't. He ran from her, hurt and confused. She'd tried to follow, but the headmaster, Mr. Sagen, had stopped her, suggesting she give him time to get used to the idea.

Reluctantly she and Paul had left. She was riddled with doubts about how she'd handled the situation. She knew he felt betrayed that she was remarrying so soon after his father's death, and angry at her for selling the house without consulting him. More than anything, she needed to straighten this out. She'd tried to call him this morning, but once again he'd refused to come to the phone. It was imperative that she go up there as soon as possible. She couldn't lose Peter. He was all she had left.

Janet paced as her nerves got the better of her. Edmund Radnor had deposited her in this room a half an hour ago, and here she still waited. It must be almost time for the ceremony. From the sounds outside, she knew the guests had all arrived. Two hundred people! She'd been astonished when Edmund had informed her of the size of the party. She took a deep breath in an attempt at control.

If Kenneth Radnor was anything like his brother, she wondered how she would survive. Not that Edmund was bad looking or obnoxious or anything like that; but he was certainly something of a dictator. Not a kind word had been offered during the ride over. He'd spent the entire time advising her of what she was to do, where she would live, how often Ken would be traveling, how she would receive payment for Peter's schooling. She'd had the distinct impression of a general giving instructions to one of his subordinates, and had suppressed a need to salute when he'd finished.

She heard the click at the door and turned in time to see a tall, dark-haired man enter the room. For a fleeting instant she thought this might be the prospective groom, but immediately shook off the thought. The man looked nothing at all like Edmund. She presumed he must be an errant guest. He walked directly toward the liquor cabinet on the opposite side of the wall, not even looking in her direction. She stood perfectly still, as if willing herself to blend into the surroundings as she observed him.

He was very tall, and his hair and eyes appeared almost black. His jaw was clenched as if in anger, or possibly frustration, as he quickly uncapped a crystal decanter and poured some amber liquid into a tumbler. He threw back his head as he very efficiently drained the contents of the glass. He was handsome, and something somewhere deep inside responded to this fact.

This feeling was somewhat of a surprise to Janet. She'd tucked that part of her life away when she'd married J.D., and had remained a virgin wife. Once in a while, when she was younger, thoughts of passion-filled romance would enter her mind. But she never indulged herself for long.

The thoughts were foolish, considering all J.D. had done for her. And if sometimes in the middle of the night her body's yearnings betrayed her, then so be it. It was a small price to pay for what she had.

Had. The word snapped Janet out of her reverie as she realized where she was. She watched as the man picked up the decanter, ready once again to fill the glass.

Suddenly Ken's peripheral vision caught a piece of creamy beige and his mind registered a presence. He turned fully toward her and studied the stunning, ethereal form across the room. *Lovely.* The word just popped into his head at the sight of her. Standing against the bay window with the late-morning sun at her back, she looked like a delicate painting, shrouded in glare, unreal and untouchable. Yet he had an irrational desire to reach out and do just that—touch.

"Hello."

Her voice was as soft as she looked, and as inviting. He felt a warmth spread through his insides that had nothing to do with the Scotch he'd just consumed. He breathed deeply to dispel it and regain control at the same time. It took him a split second to realize he was still staring and hadn't answered her.

"Hello. Sorry to barge in like this, but I needed one." He indicated the glass as he refilled it and took another sip. "Are you a guest?"

Janet hesitated a moment. "Sort of. Are you?"

He grinned. "Sort of."

They stood for a moment examining each other. Janet felt her face flush, and she watched his eyes travel slowly down her body. For all her education and supposed sophistication, she still had very little experience talking to men socially—younger men, that is. All her dealings previously were with J.D. and his friends and associates, all men who were at the very least twenty years older than she. She felt at a loss for words, and her discomfort showed on her face.

Ken couldn't believe it. She was actually blushing! Women didn't blush anymore, did they? Certainly none he knew. And judging by the full swell of her breasts, she was definitely a woman. His gaze returned to her face. No, he thought, not just a woman, a lady. A lady—very regal looking, attempting, if not succeeding, to look controlled. Her clenched hands and flushed cheeks betrayed her. And her eyes, sapphire blue and fathomless, begged for him to see more than the obvious. He suddenly realized he'd like to get to know the person hidden inside. Why, of all days, did he have to meet someone like her today?

"Would you like a drink?" he asked.

Janet nodded. "Yes, thank you. I think I would."

"What's your pleasure?"

"Scotch, if you have."

"We have. But I'm afraid there's no ice."

"Neat is fine."

She walked toward him and accepted the glass. Their fingers touched. She tried to pull the glass away, but he held on as she tugged. Janet's eyes locked with his. She felt as if he were reeling her in toward him, closer, closer. Yet in actuality they hadn't moved an inch.

"Please don't take this the wrong way, but you are a truly beautiful woman."

Her face burned at his words, and her stomach somersaulted. She tugged again at the glass and he released it. She turned away from those dark, penetrating eyes.

"I think I need one, too." She indicated the glass and took a long sip of the Scotch. It burned going down.

"Are you nervous?" he asked.

"Yes. Very."

"Am I making you nervous?"

"Yes! Very!"

She laughed out loud at his forlorn expression. He saw at once that she was teasing him, and joined in the laughter.

His laugh, strong, clear and hearty, struck a chord in Janet. Without considering the circumstances, she knew she liked him.

Against his better judgment, Ken threw caution to the wind. What he was about to do was crazy. But his emotions were involved, and he was out of practice on how to rein them in. Impulse overruled common sense.

"Would you do me the honor of having dinner with me some evening?" Ken asked.

Janet's smile froze as she acknowledged silently how very much she would *love* to have dinner with him some evening. But anything like that would be impossible. In less than an hour she would be Mrs. Kenneth Gilbert Radnor, and despite the fact that she hadn't met him, she would be obligated to play the part of his devoted wife. It was time she told the man before her who she was before they were both embarrassed.

He took her hand just then, and because the world as she knew it tilted slightly at the touch, no words flowed as she opened her mouth to speak.

When Edmund opened the door and saw his brother holding the hand of his future wife, he was clearly delighted.

"Well! I see you've both met. That saves me the trouble of awkward introductions!" he boomed.

Edmund watched the two people in front of him and continued. "We'll be getting started soon. Paul Bradly just arrived, Janet. He'll give you away as planned. Eleanor should be in any minute, and she'll explain everything else."

Edmund walked toward the liquor cabinet. "Drink? No, I see you're all set. So, what do you both think? Won't be so bad, now will it?"

Janet's hand was numb. Ken's grasp had tightened progressively with Edmund's every word and her heart was beating erratically. This man couldn't be Kenneth Radnor! She began to shake her head and her lips formed the word *no*, but no sound emerged.

Ken's jaw was locked tightly, and his eyes blazed. What a damn fool! He'd just asked his future wife out for a date! He dropped her hand abruptly and strode over to the bay window. She was supposed to be old, not this...this— He ran his hand through his hair in a common nervous gesture and stared into the garden.

"Good God!" he roared as he turned to confront Janet. "Why didn't you *say* something?"

Janet glared back at him. "Why didn't *you*?"

"What the devil—" Edmund asked, but he was immediately preempted by Eleanor's timely entrance.

"Here you all are! Kenneth, I was looking all over for you," Eleanor announced. She walked directly toward Janet. "And you must be Janet. How lovely! My, Kenneth, you've been holding out on us!"

Ken grunted something incoherent, never turning from the window.

Eleanor kissed Janet lightly on the cheek.

"Pay no attention to him, my dear. He's got the worst case of prewedding jitters I've ever seen!" Eleanor looked around at everyone, then continued, "Since no one seems anxious to introduce me, I'll do it myself. I'm Eleanor Radnor, Edmund's wife, of course, and the one to praise— or blame—for this affair today. I know you and Ken wanted a small ceremony, but it just wouldn't be a wedding without a party, now would it?''

Slowly Eleanor became aware of the uncomfortable silence in the room. "Is something wrong?"

Edmund came forward immediately. "No, nothing, darling. Just nerves. Everyone's high-strung today. I think the sooner we get this over with, the better. There's Paul. Now we can get started."

Paul Bradly entered the study and, after saying his hellos to everyone, walked to Janet's side. He bent to kiss her cheek and whispered, "How are you holding up?"

"Horribly," she answered in an equally low voice.

He patted her arm. "It'll all be over soon."

She gave him a tight smile and sat down.

"Now that everyone is here, why don't we get the minister and begin the ceremony. Eleanor?" Edmund ordered. "Will you see to that?"

Eleanor nodded and headed out the door.

Paul turned to Edmund after she'd gone. "Before we do that, Edmund, I'd like both Ken's and your signature on these."

"What is that?" Edmund asked.

"Just some papers guaranteeing that the fifteen percent of stock in question remains in Janet's name until such time as you can buy her out."

Edmund looked confused. "But of course. That's part of the deal. The stock will be owned by the Radnor family, of which Janet will be a member after today."

Paul shook his head. "I'm afraid that's not good enough, Ed. The stock must be listed under her name, Janet Demarest Radnor."

"But that would give her equal voting rights at our board meeting!"

"Correct," said Paul. "That's the way it has to be."

"Like hell it does!"

Everyone turned toward Ken, whose angry words had filled the room.

"I'm sorry if you don't like this, Ken, but I need to know that Janet will be protected."

"Protected? Protected!" Ken shouted. "She's getting my damn name, living in my house, having all her expenses paid and those of her stepson. What more do you people want—blood?"

"Please calm down, Kenneth. Shouting at Paul isn't going to solve anything." Edmund turned toward Paul. "I don't understand why you feel this is necessary."

"Theoretically you can throw her out on the street tomorrow. Once you have that stock, what guarantee do we have that you'll keep your end of the bargain?"

"Because, Mr. Bradly," Ken interrupted, "we are basically honest people. Something you've no doubt had very little experience in dealing with." He threw a scathing look to Janet.

Janet responded to that look with anger of her own. How dared he accuse her of dishonesty!

"Oh, yes, Mr. Radnor." Janet fought to control her voice. "The trust emanating from you and your brother is overwhelming! If basic honesty is the case here, why don't we call off this ridiculous marriage altogether? Support Peter and me until you can afford to buy me out. I'll be perfectly happy to reimburse you at that time. I'll even put it in writing."

Ken and Edmund looked at each other, the same thought crossing their minds simultaneously. Douglas Carmichael would find Janet easy pickings.

Janet had noted the looks they'd exchanged. "Well, is basic honesty the issue here? Or is it only *my* honesty that's in question?"

Edmund spoke first. "Give me the damn papers."

Janet and Paul shared surprised glances, but Paul complied.

When it came to Ken's turn to sign, he gazed long and hard at Janet, his eyes telling her what words never could—"you'll pay for this." She could physically feel the power of his animosity toward her. For the strangest reason, the thought of his being angry with her was intolerable. She had to make amends before the wedding took place, find some common ground before it was too late.

She moved toward him and touched his arm. He jumped back and looked at her, jaw clenched in the manner she'd already discovered was his way of keeping control.

"Mr. Radnor . . . Ken . . . please, let me explain—"

"There's no need to explain anything. The message is loud and clear." He nodded toward the papers he'd just signed.

"You don't understand—"

"I don't have to!" He turned to Edmund and Paul. "Let's get this farce over with. I've got a plane to catch in the morning."

Two

Janet peeked through the voile curtains that covered the French doors leading out to the garden. Paul Bradly was standing behind her, discussing something with Eleanor, but she tuned them out. She couldn't see where Ken had gone after storming out of the study, with Edmund hot on his trail. She watched the scene unfold before her as two young men covered the garden aisle with a white runner. The guests were seating themselves, ready to greet the bride.

The *reluctant* bride. She closed her eyes for a minute to compose herself. She couldn't go through with this, especially not now after that fiasco in the study with Ken. There had to be a way out. Had she pursued all possible solutions?

She let go of the curtain and it fell back neatly into place. She felt the tug of Paul's hand on her arm. It was time. There *was* no way out. In a few minutes she would be Mrs. Kenneth Gilbert Radnor for the period of one year. For better or worse, she was chartering new territory once again, beginning a new life much as she had eight years ago, when she had first met Peter and J.D. Only this time, she wasn't a young, orphaned girl going to meet her charge, but a grown woman going to meet the virtual stranger who would be her husband.

She accepted Paul's arm and clutched it as she walked carefully down the garden aisle in perfect time to the familiar music. The white folding chairs were meticulously arranged in straight rows, each end chair decorated with a ribboned bouquet of white orchids. The spotless runner that covered the ground made the springy grass crinkle beneath her feet as she carefully placed one foot slowly in front of the other. She kept her eyes down, looking up only occasionally as Paul guided her toward the flower-braided trellis. He was literally leading her, and she allowed him, almost as if she had no will of her own. In a very real sense that was true; for circumstances, more than any other reason, had brought her to this day. Each time she glanced up, a new crop of inquiring eyes met hers, as the invited guests scrutinized the new, soon-to-be Mrs. Radnor. *They must be wondering what ever made him ask me to marry him in the first place. If they only knew!*

If Janet wondered what the guests thought of her, Ken didn't. He knew. His eyes were fixed on her as she approached him seemingly in slow motion. Try as he might, he couldn't look away. She *was* beautiful. And she looked so demure, so vulnerable. He watched her glance briefly at the guests, then lower her eyes again. In a few more minutes, this woman would be his wife. A bittersweet pain twisted his stomach at the thought; his heart began to pound. He wanted to reach out, meet her halfway down the aisle and take her in his arms. He also wanted to somehow punish her for what she was doing to him.

As these conflicting thoughts warred within him, she arrived at his side. Paul gently released her hand and gave it into Ken's. He tucked her arm within his and covered her hand with his own. Her face was concealed by the wide brim of her hat as Ken looked down at her. Janet turned and looked up at him inquiringly, almost as if he'd spoken her name. Filled with innocence, her large, blue eyes entreated him, and for a brief moment, Ken was enchanted, mesmerized, forgetting who she was, who he was and how they came to be there.

Janet smiled, a tentative, tremulous smile meant only as an offering of peace, but at the same time unknowingly sensual and seductive. Ken froze, misinterpreting the smile not as one of truce, but of triumph. He hardened his heart. Innocent, indeed! There was no such thing as an innocent woman. Ken turned his head quickly and nodded toward the minister to begin the ceremony.

Janet released the deep breath she'd been holding and swallowed. For a moment, all pretense disappeared. His face had seemed calm, his eyes receptive. The charming man in the study had returned for that split second. But then he turned to stone again. She watched as he clenched his jaw. He removed his hand from hers. Digging her nails into the material of his jacket, she gave her attention to the minister. What had she done?

Janet tried to pay attention to what the minister was saying, but the words were meaningless. He spoke of loving, of honoring each other, of total union and commitment, of a life's partnership—none of which had anything to do with this marriage. Their partnership, if one could call it that, was based on stocks and money, and would probably not even last the year. It seemed a shame to waste those words and the beautiful, cloudless day.

She gave the expected responses correctly and on time, without a quiver in her voice. Yet her mind wandered to another time, another day when she had married J.D. In contrast, that day had produced a feeling of contentment, of joy and coming home. She felt none of those things now, only emptiness and fear, especially of the future and what living with this man would mean.

When Ken put his hand on hers, she realized it was time for the ring. Her left hand shook as she held it out to him. She heard his annoyed, sharp intake of breath and muttered words, and realized the reason. She'd forgotten to take off J.D.'s wedding band. Quickly Ken slipped it off and pocketed it before placing the intricately carved antique gold band on her hand. It was slightly large, but very, very beautiful. She sensed it must have been his mother's. As she admired it, she knew that after the year was up, she would have to give it back. Like the Radnor name, it was only on loan to her.

This was all too much. As the minister pronounced them husband and wife, she felt the tears gather in her eyes. The minister smiled and touched Ken's arm.

"You may kiss your bride."

Ken turned her until she was facing him, intending to give her a peck on the cheek for the benefit of the audience. But when Janet raised her face to him, and those huge, sapphire eyes shimmered with unshed, sparkling tears, an explosion ripped through him, blotting out all thought save one. This woman was his wife. A protective urge surfaced from where he did not know, and he found himself gently wrapping his arms around her as he pulled her closer. His lips sought hers, softly, uncertain of her response. He felt her relax against him, and drew her tighter still, holding her securely in the nest of his arms as she reached up around his neck, gripping him for support.

They touched, ever so lightly at first, and she sighed against his mouth, her breath warm and sweet and so inviting. Ken groaned and captured her lips with his own, no longer gentle but demanding, taking all she was willing to give. She arched into him and their bodies strained together. They clung to each other as their senses reeled.

No one had ever tasted like this, Ken thought, felt like this before. He was drowning, yet he didn't give a damn.

A persistent cough registered somewhere in his rapidly diminishing consciousness, but Ken didn't react until a hand tapped his shoulder rather forcefully. He opened his eyes, and with a jolt realized where he was. Two hundred guests grinned knowingly at him. He jumped back and released Janet so quickly she lost her balance and he had to grab her arms to steady her. In doing so, he caught a glimpse of her slightly swollen lips. Edmund leaned over and thrust a clean white handkerchief in front of him. Ken dutifully wiped the smudge of lipstick from his mouth as he attempted to capture Janet's eye. He needed to see the expression on her face, needed to know if that one electrifying kiss had affected her as strongly as it had him. He felt like the walking wounded. What the hell had happened?

But it was too late. Eleanor was at Janet's side, adjusting her makeup with a tissue as she pulled her toward the guests beginning to congregate around the trellis.

Janet was physically shaken. Her hands were like ice and hung clenched at her sides as people she didn't know came up to offer their congratulations. She smiled and accepted them as graciously as possible, all the while desperately trying to avoid Ken's eyes. She knew that if he saw her face, he would know how deeply his kiss had disturbed her.

No one had ever kissed her that way. What was worse, she had never kissed anyone *back* that way! It took her totally by surprise. It frightened her. It confused her. But most of all, it excited her.

Ken was off to the other side, accepting his share of good wishes, as Edmund moved closer to him.

"What was that little display all about?" Edmund asked.

Ken didn't pretend to misunderstand his brother's question. Summoning a bit of male bravado, as well as his normal voice, he answered, "Just teaching the lady a little lesson."

Edmund's eyebrows shot up. "Many more lessons like that one, dear brother, and we can kiss the grounds for annulment goodbye!"

Ken threw him a withering look, but was stopped from a verbal reply by Eleanor's insistence that they all remove themselves from the flower garden. The servants were waiting to disassemble the chairs to make more room for the party. Eleanor ushered them toward a pond nestled in a small copse at the easterly end of the grounds. With an arm around both Ken and Janet, she led them toward a short, fat, rather comical-looking man with an enormous array of camera equipment hanging around his neck, as well as strewn about his feet.

Wedding pictures? Janet shook her head, not quite believing anyone in this family would seriously want to preserve this day for posterity. But preserve it they would, as she allowed Eleanor to situate her in the center of the group picture. The photographer instructed one person or another to move this way or that, incline a head, lift a chin and most of all, smile, smile, smile! He took his time, orchestrating pose after pose, until Janet felt she was involved in a publicity layout for a major motion picture production rather than a wedding album. Her lips were so pulled and drawn from smiling she felt they would split, and her jaw ached. Each smile was artificial, and she knew that once the pictures were developed, the look would be the same. She wondered how Ken was bearing up, but since that devastating kiss after the ceremony, she hadn't so much as glanced his way, more afraid than anything that he would see the look in her eyes. And what was that look? she wondered. Desire? Passion? Awe?

By the time Ken and Janet returned to the garden, the party was in full swing. People were walking around, sipping champagne and nibbling hors d'oeuvres as tuxedoed waiters wove inconspicuously through the crowd.

The garden was a beautifully manicured area of lush green grass, so soft and thick it felt as though she were walking on a deep, plush carpet. The shrubbery was well tended, picture perfect. People touched random plants and shrubs, rubbing the leaves as if trying to discern if they were real. Off to the side nearer the house was a huge tent that enclosed tables and chairs, as well as an extremely long buffet table laden with both hot and cold food. There was even a roasted suckling pig complete with the traditional apple in its mouth. Off in another corner stood a well-stocked bar, catering to anyone who didn't find the free-flowing champagne to their liking.

Janet was overwhelmed. She'd been to lavish affairs with J.D. on occasion, but never one so opulent as this. She knew the Radnor family was wealthy, and certainly didn't begrudge their spending their money as they saw fit. But why for this? This affair was a celebration of the highest sorts. Under different circumstances, she would have been flattered, even overjoyed, that her new husband and his family chose to present her to their friends and business associates in such a splendid showcase. Yet the way things stood, the entire affair only added to her suspicion.

Ken lifted two champagne glasses from a moving tray. He noticed Janet's rapt expression as he handed her a glass. "Pretty impressive display, isn't it?" he asked.

"Yes, it is. Too impressive, in fact."

"Don't you think you deserve it?"

"That's not the point," she answered his taunt, staring directly into his deep, dark eyes.

"Then what is, Mrs. Radnor?"

Janet started as he addressed her by her new name. She noticed the glint in his eyes and knew he'd successfully put her in her place.

"The point, *Mr. Radnor*, is that this wedding—and our marriage, I might add—is a sham. I fail to see why you'd want to celebrate it."

Ken's expression sobered. She saw no anger, only resignation.

"It's Eleanor's doing. She's such a romantic. Ed and I didn't have the heart—or the nerve—to stop her. She never had a chance to do this for me the first time around and always felt cheated."

"First time?" Janet croaked. For some reason the words stuck in her throat.

"Why, yes. I was married before. I thought you knew."

Janet shook her head, not trusting her voice. Why did his having been married before bother her? "What happened?" she asked finally.

"Divorced. Years ago. It was one of those things. We eloped during a college football weekend. The family never forgave me."

"Did you love her?" Now why did she ask that? Janet glanced around at the crowd, not able to look at Ken's face, afraid of what she might see there.

Ken cupped her chin in his hand, and turned her face to meet his eyes. "Does it matter to you?" he asked softly.

"No, of course not! What do I care how many wives or lovers you've had?"

His face turned hard again and he dropped his hand. "Then why did you ask?"

"I don't know. It seemed like the thing to say."

"You are one strange lady, Mrs. Radnor!"

She glared at him. "*I'm* strange?" Her voice was shrill even in her own ears. Realizing she was amid a crowd of people, she lowered it to a harsh whisper. "That's a laugh! This—" she swept her hand around to indicate the party "—is the *strangest* thing I've ever seen! This wedding had to have cost enough to support Peter and me for at least a year! Why didn't you save yourself time and aggravation and just give me the money instead of having this—what was it you so charmingly called it? Oh, yes, a farce—this farce?"

His jaw was tight, his expression hard and his eyes implacable. He grabbed hold of her wrist and drew her closer to him, their faces only inches apart.

"Money. That's really all you're interested in, isn't it? I'll have to remember to kick myself every so often so I don't forget!"

She extricated her hand from his grasp. "Don't bother. I'll be happy to kick you periodically as a reminder!"

She turned to walk away as regally as possible for the benefit of the smiling guests, but Ken followed close behind.

"Wait!"

She stopped and whirled around, a haughty expression on her face. He was angry, and while one small part of her regretted that, she felt justified.

Ken's face was frozen in a fake smile as he grinned at those around them. He put his hand to the small of her back and ushered her off to the side where they could have a degree of privacy.

"What is it?" she asked.

The fire in his eyes was the only barometer of his feelings. Her anger dissipated. He was so handsome, so masculine. His chiseled features beckoned to her to reach out and touch. She wanted to rub that hint of a dimple in his chin. Of its own volition, her hand reached up to caress that tense jaw, but his grip interrupted the action midway.

"Here," he said, placing something in her palm. He closed his fist over it. "You forgot something, Mrs. Radnor."

He squeezed her fist shut, digging the object into her soft flesh. Then, with one last scathing look, he released her hand, turned and walked away, leaving her alone in the corner, staring into various pairs of curious, strange eyes.

She opened her hand, and unbidden tears formed as she stared at its contents. There, in the soft glow of afternoon, sparkled J.D.'s wedding ring.

Three

———

There you are, my dear!'' Eleanor called out to her. ''Come this way and let me bring you around. Everyone's dying to meet you.''

Janet groaned inwardly, but obediently followed Eleanor. She looked around for Ken, but he was nowhere to be seen. She had to stop this. She'd known him only a matter of hours and he was fast becoming an obsession. She needed to find the best way to deal with the man who was so clearly out of her league. He was sophisticated, sarcastic, demanding, and nothing like anyone she'd ever dealt with before. The easiest course was to ignore him. She closed her eyes briefly and repeated the drill in her head. *He doesn't exist*.

With the thought solidly implanted in her mind, Janet reached into her inner reserve of charm and withdrew a smile for the new group of people to whom Eleanor was introducing her. An hour later, she was exhausted and sure there wasn't one soul left who hadn't received her most heartfelt smile and firm handshake. It seemed as if Eleanor was dragging rather than leading her. Janet was about to ask for a respite, when she noticed a tall red-haired man standing off to the side with a very attractive woman. He was waving to Eleanor to join them.

"Oh, dear," Eleanor said. "I'd forgotten about him. And her." She sighed at Janet's perplexed expression. "It's just as well you don't understand at the moment, Janet. Come. It's best to get this over with now."

Eleanor led her toward the couple. As she extended her hand, the tall man engulfed it in his own very large ones.

"Eleanor! How wonderful to see you! And thank you for inviting me to this fabulous celebration." He growled in a deep, warm voice, "I thought I was persona non grata around here."

"Douglas! Don't be silly. Whatever business differences you have with Edmund are left at the front door. You know that. We've all been friends for years!"

"Well, I thank you sincerely, Eleanor, for that kind welcome. But please, introduce us to this beautiful bride!"

Janet was studying the man as he spoke. He was as tall as Ken, but much bigger, broader. His auburn hair and sparkling blue eyes were set off by a ruddy complexion, which suggested that he worked outdoors, or at least spent a great deal of time there. His suit was well cut and expensive, but seemed somehow misplaced on his large frame. His eyes bored into hers as he extended his hand for Eleanor's introduction.

"Janet, this is Douglas Carmichael, an old friend and business associate of the Radnors. And this lovely young woman with him is Johanna Cassidy."

"Congratulations on your marriage. It was quite a coup trapping the elusive Kenneth Radnor. We all thought him a lost cause, virtually unattainable," Johanna purred.

Janet bristled beneath the sarcasm. The woman had a low, smoky, seductive voice some try, but fail, to imitate. The sound sent chills up Janet's back.

"You can't know Kenneth very well if you think he could be *trapped* by anyone," Eleanor commented. "He does nothing against his will." She turned to smile at Janet. "One has only to look at them together to know it was a love match." She laughed and looked back at the other couple. "Why, Edmund had to practically pry them apart at the altar!"

Janet almost choked on her sip of champagne as she blushed to her roots. She wondered at Eleanor's quick defense of her. As she tried to determine exactly what was going on, she caught the twinkle in Douglas's eyes.

"Excuse me," Johanna said. "There's Ken. I must congratulate him personally."

Johanna took off at a brisk pace and headed straight toward the bar, where Ken was speaking to a group of men. At the same moment, an elderly matron waved to Eleanor.

"You'll have to excuse me, also, I'm afraid. There's Mrs. Naughton, my garden club chairlady. I must speak to her. Janet? Will you be all right?"

Before Janet could open her mouth, Douglas replied, "Go along, Eleanor. I'll be happy to entertain Mrs. Radnor, if she'll allow."

At Janet's nod, Eleanor was off, leaving her alone with this handsome and definitely unsettling man. She lifted the champagne glass to take another sip as she glanced around at the crowd. Her hand froze in midair as she spotted Johanna. Her long slim arms were wrapped possessively around Ken's neck. She was smiling up at him, her body leaning into his. Ken's hands were at her waist, either supporting her or keeping some sort of distance between them, Janet couldn't tell which. However, by the look on his face—a kind of rapt expression—Janet didn't think he'd ever thrown her out of bed. The question was, would he now that he was married?

Janet tried to tell herself it shouldn't bother her, that she had no right to ask or expect anything of him in this arrangement. If he was having an affair with Johanna, why not continue it? Their marriage was a business deal, pure and simple, and his personal life was his own.

Yet watching them embrace turned her stomach. *He doesn't belong to you, Janet,* she told herself. He was a free agent—and so was she. Her mind churned with the thoughts. She was so busy with her contemplation, she didn't hear Douglas address her.

"What? Pardon me, Mr. Carmichael, my mind was elsewhere."

Douglas looked in the direction of Johanna and Ken, who were now separated and talking companionably.

"Yes," he said. "I can see where it was."

She noticed that twinkle back in his eyes.

"Don't let Johanna get to you. She planned all this very carefully. She's pretending to nurse a broken heart."

"Are they lovers?" Janet asked.

Douglas's face registered surprise at her question. "Lovers? I really don't know. Could be, I suppose. They dated a while back, but I tend to think that whatever affair they had took place more in Johanna's mind than in fact. She's had a 'thing' for Ken for years. Even before Marcia."

"Marcia? His first wife?"

Douglas nodded. "For a bride, you seem to know very little about your new husband."

Janet felt him scrutinize her as if attempting to read her mind.

"It's true," she answered. "We don't know each other very well."

"You took us all by surprise, I must say. No one even knew Ken was seriously dating, let alone contemplating marriage."

"Let's just chalk it up to a whirlwind courtship." Janet lowered her gaze and stared into the glass, unable to look this man in the face with her blatant lie.

Douglas lifted her chin, forcing her to look at him. "Janet, you seem to be a very sweet person, and very vulnerable. I don't know exactly what's going on here, and you don't seem willing to talk about it, but if you ever do, promise me you'll think of me. I can be a very sympathetic shoulder to cry on, especially where the Radnors are concerned." He rubbed her chin gently with his thumb. "And, honey, you look as if you may be needing one."

His kindness should have reassured Janet, but it accomplished the opposite. She fought the burning tears but couldn't control them as they began to well up in her eyes. Douglas cupped her face in his huge hands as his thumbs stroked the corners of her eyes, wiping away the slight trace of tears.

"Hey," he said softly. "Don't—"

"I see you've met my wife, Carmichael."

Ken's voice rang out loud and clear. Both she and Douglas jumped, and he dropped his hands from her face. Janet felt as if they had been caught with their hands in the cookie jar, and by the look on Ken's face, he thought so, too.

"Hello, Ken. We were just discussing your marriage." Douglas's smile was calm and sincere as he extended his hand toward Ken. "Congratulations, by the way."

Ken didn't extend his hand in return, and Douglas withdrew awkwardly. Janet knew Ken was angry by that increasingly familiar clenched jaw of his. She was grateful that Douglas Carmichael had backed off without a confrontation, more for her sake than for his own. She sensed something very wrong between the two men that went far deeper than this recent episode. She nodded as Douglas excused himself and walked away. But instinctively she knew this wouldn't be the last they saw of him.

Janet met Ken's angry gaze with one of her own.

"That was so rude! He appears to be a very nice—"

"Appearances can be deceiving," Ken interrupted. "What was he saying to you?" It was a demand, not a request.

"What do you mean? We were talking, that's all. Small talk. You have a nerve—"

"That didn't look like small talk to me! He looked as if he was going to kiss you! For heaven's sake, you're supposed to be my wife. Don't you care what people think, seeing you hiding in the corner with some man in what certainly looked like an intimate situation!"

Janet was seething. "Intimate situation! *You* should talk! Standing out there in the open, over by the bar with that . . . that woman—or should I say mistress?—hanging all over you! At least I had the decency to be in the corner," she groaned. "What am I saying? I wasn't doing anything! The man was only being kind. I was tired and more than a little upset, and he tried to comfort me. Why am I even bothering to tell this to you? I don't owe you any explanations!"

Janet started to stalk away. Ken grabbed her wrist and pulled her back so abruptly they bumped. There they stood, joined hip to hip and glaring at each other.

"You're my wife."

"And you're my husband!"

Ken stared for a moment longer, took a deep breath and released her arm. "Okay. You're right. I overreacted. Let's make a pact, shall we? For the next year, or however long this takes, we won't embarrass each other in public. How's that?"

Janet stepped away, putting much-needed distance between them. "And in private?"

"Janet," he warned, "don't—"

"Don't what? Don't think? Don't feel? Just act—or react, I should say. I don't know how I'm going to live like this!"

"We both agreed that this was the best way."

"Yes, but I'm beginning to regret that decision immensely."

Ken looked at the ground for a moment, then took hold of her hand. He slowly caressed her knuckles as he marveled at how small and delicate her hand was. This wasn't going as he'd planned, hadn't from the very first minute he'd seen her outlined against the bay window in the study. Why did he react so strongly to seeing her and Carmichael together? If this "marriage" was going to have half a chance, he was going to have to get himself under control where she was concerned. But damn, the woman could rile him! He took a deep breath and expelled it as he rolled his eyes heavenward for an answer. Control, he told himself. First and foremost, control.

"Look, I'm sorry. I'll try not to go overboard in the future. We're off to a bad start today, and for that I apologize. Let's do our best to enjoy the rest of the day, okay?"

Janet slowly withdrew her hand from his. His words warmed her, but his touch was disturbing. Yet more than anything she wanted to accept the olive branch he was offering. She was more confused than ever by her roller-coaster emotions.

"Yes, fine," she said as she turned her head toward the tented area. "Can we get something to eat? I'm starved."

"So am I. Come on," Ken said with a smile.

For the second time that day she was unnerved by the transformation his face undertook when he smiled. The effect was as complete as if he'd cast out a tightly woven net, caught her and pulled her in. But that wasn't the worse part. The worse part was that she couldn't think of anywhere she would rather be. She was very attracted to him, and under the circumstances, that attraction was not only stupid, it was dangerous.

He led her through the garden to the food line. They chatted amiably with the guests as they loaded their plates with salads, meats and vegetables. She didn't realize how truly hungry she was until the sight and smell of all the appetizing dishes invaded her senses. The two of them found an empty table and sat, concentrating on their dinner rather than each other. People walked by without interrupting, with only a passing word or gesture, seeming to think the newlyweds preferred their privacy. Oddly enough, they were right.

Janet was strangely content to be alone with Ken. When he was quiet, his presence reassured her. There was an innate strength in him that transmitted itself to her. She studied his face, his hands, his dark wavy hair. He was so easy to look at. She could easily understand Johanna's consternation over their marriage. If he was hers, truly hers, she would find it hard, almost impossible to lose him. But he wasn't. Even though she shared his name, she had no right to share anything more. That was the bargain. She sighed inwardly and put down her fork. How would this all end? Her thoughts and feelings frightened her, but at the same time, the year looming ahead of her gave her a rush of excitement the likes of which she had never experienced.

Ken looked up and their gazes locked. He wondered what she was thinking. She was studying him; he'd felt it while he was eating. What did she think of him? He wished he knew. Was she only interested in the money? He knew she'd entered into this agreement to support her stepson, or at least that's what he'd been led to believe. But were her motives all so unselfish? She had to be getting *something* out of this. It made him angry to think of her as purely mercenary, and that bothered him, too. Emotions he didn't ever remember experiencing had been surfacing fast and furious since the moment they'd met. He wanted to trust her, but would she agree to anything if the price was right? That thought brought Douglas Carmichael back to mind.

"What did Carmichael offer you?" The words tumbled out of his mouth before he could stop them.

"Offer me? What are you talking about?"

All good intentions gone, he persisted. "Don't play games, Janet. We both know I'm talking about the stock."

Janet's shock registered on her face. She had no idea what he meant.

"We didn't talk about the stock. I didn't tell him I own any, so I don't suppose he even knows. Unless you've told him."

"Don't be ridiculous! Carmichael's been after us for years, trying to gain a seat on our board of directors."

"Well, how in the world was I supposed to know that?"

"Well, now I'm telling you."

"What *is* it between you two? You're so hostile toward him."

"You'd be hostile, too, if he did the things to your family that he's done to mine."

"Such as?"

"I'd really rather not get into it now."

"Why not? Whatever happened in the past is affecting me now. I think I have a right to know."

Ken gritted his teeth. She watched him weigh how much to tell her.

"He stole a company out from under us. It was a deal my father worked long and hard on for years. He found out somehow, and outbid us. My father never recovered from the loss. He died of a heart attack soon after." Ken pushed his plate away, his appetite lost as the memory returned. "That's your 'nice' Mr. Carmichael."

Somehow Janet knew there was more to it than this, but felt it wise to accept Ken's explanation at the moment. She would find out the rest another time.

"So," she began, her voice wary. "What exactly are you telling me, Ken?"

"I'm telling you to keep away from him. If and when he finds out you own part of the corporation, he'll be hot on your trail."

She bristled under his order. "Don't tell me whom I can or can't talk with, Ken. I won't stand for you screening my friends."

"Carmichael is no friend. He'll only seem to be to get what he wants."

"We'll see," she said as she resumed eating, subject closed as far as she was concerned.

Ken slammed his fist down on the table. "Don't 'we'll see' me, Janet! Stay away from him!"

Janet's shock at his reaction showed on her face, but she wasn't about to let Ken get the upper hand in this matter, not so soon into what she already knew was going to be a difficult relationship. She was just about to tell him off, when Eleanor found them.

"It's time to cut the cake."

They both stood, glaring at each other as Eleanor escorted her reluctant charges to the main table, where a seven-tier cake awaited them.

"Hasn't the day been splendid?" Eleanor asked brightly, completely oblivious to the tension between the two.

Janet smiled a short, tight smile at the woman and wondered where she got her energy.

Eleanor patted her arm. "It's almost over, dear. I know how trying today must be for you. Let's cut the cake and then soon after, you and Kenneth can be on your way."

Janet glanced over Eleanor's head toward Ken. Off to where? she thought. Surely she wasn't talking about a honeymoon! Ken shook his head, understanding her unasked question and reassuring her with his look. Janet blew out a relieved breath and joined Ken at the table.

The cake-cutting ceremony was disgustingly traditional, complete with the bride and groom feeding each other. Janet wanted to stuff the entire bottom tier down Ken's throat, and knew beyond the shadow of a doubt that he wished to do the same to her.

Four

The day was over, finally. It had been the longest day of her life as far as Janet was concerned. She sat down in the overstuffed armchair near the fireplace and looked around the room to which Eleanor had directed her. It wasn't a very large room, but definitely masculine in decor. The rug was a deep, rich chocolate brown and the armchair, couch and love seat a light tan velvet. The furniture was arranged around the fireplace in a cozy semicircle. There was a rolling service bar, seemingly well stocked, in the corner. Off to the other side of the room stood an antique desk of rich mahogany with a straight-backed chair. The desk was cluttered with papers and folders, indicating it wasn't just for decoration.

On the opposite wall was a small efficiency kitchen. It boasted a two-burner stove and a miniature refrigerator under two cabinets. A small coffee machine sat on top of the work counter. All the comforts of home, Janet mused as her gaze swung back toward the far left. There stood a bookcase and stereo with two additional arched doorways, which she assumed led into the bedroom and bath. It was a complete apartment, and she was sure it was Ken's. Where was he sleeping tonight? She knew he had a plane to catch first thing in the morning for California. He'd certainly reminded her of that fact enough times!

Well, it didn't matter. The strange and disturbing wedding was over. Janet was so overtired, she didn't want to think about the events of the day right now. She was sure the reality of it all would come crashing down on her tomorrow. At this moment, all she wanted was a nice warm bath and bed, in that order. With what seemed to her a superhuman effort, she pushed herself out of the very comfortable chair and headed for one of the doorways.

The first revealed a tiny room, not quite a den, with a love seat and recliner facing a portable television. A combination magazine rack-table lamp stood next to the chair. She leaned on the doorjamb and smiled. If she had to live in this place for a year, she could at least look forward to this small alcove for relaxation as well as getting away from the "family."

Janet headed toward the other doorway and entered the bedroom. She switched on the lamp and looked around. The room was enormous. And so was the bed. The huge, heavy oak four-poster dominated the room, dwarfing the highboy and armoire in comparison. The high, old-fashioned bed would be perfectly proportioned to Ken's large body. To Janet's overly tired eyes, it would be the sweetest climb she'd ever made.

She looked around and spotted her one small overnight case in the corner of the room. The remainder of her clothing and personal articles would arrive tomorrow. Janet began to undress, finding a walk-in closet as she roamed around the room, removing her dress, shoes and stockings. She pushed back some of Ken's suits and made room to hang her dress. She left her shoes neatly beneath it and closed the door.

Picking up her overnight case, she made her way into the bathroom. It was also oversize, with an inviting antique claw-foot bathtub. She ran the water and glanced quickly in the mirror before returning to the bedroom. After she'd efficiently turned the bed down, she returned to the bathroom and closed the door.

Janet pinned her hair up haphazardly with a large barrette she'd had since adolescence, one of those fake tortoiseshell ones she somehow could never bring herself to part with. As the room began to steam up, she completed undressing. The hot water felt heavenly as she gradually submerged herself in it. She sighed, and the tensions of the day slipped away as her muscles unknotted and relaxed. It would be easy to fall asleep, soothed by the lapping water. As she angled down to rest her head on the curved lip of the tub, she closed her eyes and did just that.

Ken walked into his apartment, simultaneously shrugging out of his jacket, tugging his shirttails out of his pants and kicking off his shoes. He was exhausted. The last-minute sermon from Edmund on Carmichael, Janet, the meetings on the coast and a million other minute details was the last straw. He was numb, and it had been a hell of a long day. The wedding took much more energy than he'd ever thought he would expend for such an occasion. All the tension, the endless talking, chatting, polite conversation, coupled with Eleanor's perfectly timed choreography of events, made him feel like a puppet on a string, a mindless fool.

And the dancing! Eleanor had had to hire that stupid band, had had to go the whole horrible route with a wedding song and everything! What was that insipid little love ballad she'd picked? Unless Janet had picked it. He couldn't remember the words, but the melody was still swirling in his head, hauntingly replaying itself in his mind. He did remember the feel of Janet's body next to his, the way she'd brushed against him. He felt himself respond to the vivid memory almost as quickly as he had on the dance floor— Enough!

He stood and walked over to the service bar and poured himself a short brandy, then gracelessly collapsed onto the love seat, his stockinged feet resting on the coffee table as he took a large gulp. He held it in his mouth and swished it around as one would do with a fine wine. It burned his tongue, but felt good as he slowly allowed the liquid to trickle down his throat. No, Janet wouldn't have picked that song. She was definitely hostile, as against this marriage as he was. He was sure the silly, romantic moment was Eleanor's idea. But as he closed his eyes and rested his head against the cushions, his imagination went wild and he not only felt Janet's soft body flush up against his own, but could almost smell her soft, beguiling perfume, as well. It wasn't sweet as some were, but subtle, alluring, distinctly her own, not a famous brand or even recognizable. He wondered where the scent originated. He breathed deeply, trying to locate its source, dispel it; yet it clung in his nostrils in much the same way the tune repeated itself in his mind.

She was so feminine. She'd fitted perfectly in his arms, her full breasts just grazing his chest. He'd tried not to hold her too tightly, but it had taken all his control not to crush her to him, not to touch her the way he truly wanted to touch her, not to see if she was really as soft as she looked. And then there was that kiss at the altar...

Ken opened his eyes and sat up. Stop it! he ordered himself, almost growling out loud with anger. Edmund was right. He would never make it through this year unless he got this attraction under control. That had been the long and short of his beloved brother's lecture downstairs. He felt like a schoolboy being taken to task.

Lord, he was angry! Edmund was acting as if he were some teenager with galloping hormones. The corporation was just as important to him as it was to Edmund and the rest of the family. Did Ed really think he would do anything to jeopardize what he'd worked so hard for all these years, even to the exclusion of any social life? No, Edmund was wrong. He could, and would, pull this off. With all the traveling he did, the year would fly by, and then she would be gone.

He stood and walked toward the bedroom. He sat on the edge of the bed, pulling off his socks and pants. Why did that thought give him a sinking feeling in the pit of his stomach? He would be damn glad when that irritating woman disappeared from his life. He didn't need her big doe eyes looking up at him, beseeching, enchanting, *or* condemning! He didn't owe her a thing!

He'd sacrificed a lot for his family and ever since this harebrained scheme had begun to take over his life he'd been neglecting even more. He rubbed a hand over his flat abdomen, making a mental note to get back to the gym for his regular exercise program. Yes, once he got back into his normal routine, he would hardly have time to remember he was married!

With that thought firmly in place he headed for the bathroom. Maybe a shower would clear Janet from his head.

* * *

Janet opened her eyes suddenly and listened intently for a repeat of whatever sound had woken her. She sat up in the bath. The water was cool and no longer comfortable. She rose and stepped onto the thick-pile rug near the tub, grabbing the big bath towel that was hanging on the rack. She clutched the towel to her chest and bent to let the water drain out of the tub.

It was the all-too-brief sight of a well-rounded derriere that greeted Ken as he swung open the bathroom door. Janet felt the cool air on her back almost at the same moment she heard the door. With a barely audible "Oh!" she swung around and faced a delighted Ken.

At least, he looked delighted. Or amused. Or idiotic. She wasn't sure which one. He just seemed to stand there staring at her with the strangest look on his face, almost a half smile. Or smirk. Or grimace. Or *something*. Lord, he could have been in pain.

They drank each other in with their eyes. Janet felt the blush that always lurked so close to the surface begin to spread its red glow to her slightly damp face. His gaze bored into hers, and she heard a whimper—soft, low, desperate. It took a second to realize the sound had come from herself, because she'd stopped staring at his face and had glanced down to his boldly vital body. It stopped her cold. His slight briefs left absolutely nothing to the imagination, but try as she might, she couldn't tear her eyes away from his firm thighs or what was highlighted so blatantly between them.

A chill returned her to the present, and she realized that she didn't even have the towel wrapped around her but was clutching it to her breasts for dear life. She hastily lowered her eyes and quickly pulled the downy soft cloth around herself, carefully tucking the edge in front, between her breasts.

"What are you doing here?" she asked.

It took Ken a moment to answer. She glanced up to see what was wrong. Nothing was wrong. He was still staring at her in that strange, compelling way.

"Uh, I was just about to ask you the same thing."

"I was shown to these rooms," she said. "I was under the impression this was where I would be staying."

"These are my rooms."

"That is obvious. It's also obvious that you weren't supposed to be staying here tonight."

He saw her anger rise to the surface. He didn't want to provoke her—at least not in that way.

"I'm sorry. I didn't see your luggage, or I would have known you were using these rooms. I guess I assumed you'd be in the guest wing. Please accept my apologies for interrupting you."

Janet watched his face. His tone of voice was contrite and he seemed sincere. Her hostility dissipated. The mistake was, after all, understandable.

"It's all right." She walked toward the door and he moved slightly to make room for her to pass.

But as she made contact with him, he dropped his arm across the doorway, blocking her. She turned her head to question him. His answering gaze froze her to the spot. Her stomach muscles knotted as his warm breath stirred the wisps of hair around her forehead. She knew she should push past him, but for the life of her she couldn't. She was incapable of rational thought, or even motion for that matter. All she could do was stand there, waiting for whatever he was planning to do, and more than ready for it.

Ken raised his hand and pulled the barrette out of her hair. She faintly heard it fall onto the tile floor. He smoothed out the tangles in her hair with his fingers. Then he lowered his head in a slow, inevitable descent toward hers. She raised her face to meet him halfway.

"I have to know," he whispered, "if it was real."

That he was referring to their impassioned kiss at the altar, she had no doubt. Yet all other coherent thought fled as he gently brushed his lips across hers. He rubbed them back and forth, his breath mingling with hers to moisten her lips and his, until the final moment when he claimed her mouth totally. She swayed into him and he dropped his arm and encircled her waist. He shifted his body and leaned against the doorjamb, bringing her closer to him, into him, his arms completely filled with her.

He opened his mouth wider to deepen the kiss, his tongue entering her mouth, seeking and finding hers. He tasted of brandy, and her senses reeled under the assault. He was devouring her, nipping at her lips, pulling on her tongue, delving deeper into her mouth with his own. She had never, ever been kissed like this; nor had she ever imagined it. It was intoxicating. He felt so good, so strong, so vital. She moved her hands around his back and touched the solid straining muscles. He slipped his hands from her waist to cup her buttocks, almost lifting her off the floor in the process.

That he was thoroughly aroused was crystal clear, especially noticeable with only the slight bits of cloth between them. Janet moved her body against his, luxuriating in the sensations. She wanted to get as close as possible. She wanted to discard the offensive fabric and feel him, all of him, without any barriers. She wanted more, much more than this kissing. She wanted him to touch her, caress her in the most primitive, elemental ways of men and women.

Ken broke the kiss, but kept his lips a breath away from hers as he sighed her name. He left a trail of scorching nips down her throat, her neck, her collarbone and the tiny indentation in between. She ran her fingers through his hair, holding his head, guiding him as he feasted.

"Janet?"

It was a loaded question, with only one possible answer as far as she was concerned. Janet wanted him desperately. Never before had she experienced this fascination for a man. It was as if she were a small, helpless moth fluttering around this fierce, gigantic flame. She needed him, to be his, in every way, any way, he would have her.

He was her husband. She wanted more than anything else in the world to be his wife.

"Ken," she whispered in his ear. "Yes, oh, please."

He lifted her into his arms so quickly she lost her breath. Giving her no time to recant, he covered her mouth once again with his mouth. He carried her into the bedroom and laid her down gently on the bed, the king-size pillow cradling her head. Ken sat back and stared at her for a long, intense moment. She met his gaze and held it. He saw her swollen lips pout and he stopped himself from kissing her again. He would, of course, but not now. Now he wanted to look his fill and see for himself if she was really as perfect as he'd imagined.

In slow motion, he easily tugged the towel free. He felt his hands shake as he carefully folded back first one side, then the other. All the while his eyes never left hers as he savored the anticipation, the thrill of seeing, of touching her breasts. He lowered his eyes and stared in delight at the sight. A sprinkling of warmth descended on his body and centered in his loins as he reached out with both hands to touch her, filling each hand almost to overflowing. He flicked his thumbs across her nipples ever so gently and was rewarded with a soft moan.

Janet closed her eyes, floating in a sea of sensation as his slightly rough palms caressed her breasts. When she opened her eyes again, Ken's penetrating black gaze was there to meet her, his eyes intent, fathomless and passionate.

"You're so beautiful," he said. "More so than I ever imagined."

"You've imagined me like this?"

He continued his gentle play and smiled dreamily. "Oh, yes. All day, in fact, ever since I first saw you standing in the study wrapped in sunlight."

Janet raised her hands and brought his head down to her. "Kiss me."

He obliged with pleasure, his hands never leaving her breasts as he captured her lips once again. He kissed her again and again, his tongue delving deeply, almost, she thought, into the recesses of her soul. She felt his heart thudding strongly as she caressed the thick mat of dark curls on his chest. When she urged him closer, he moved his body onto hers, freeing his hands to roam over her entire body. His mouth left hers and he began to explore her neck and throat, licking lightly, rubbing his wonderfully abrasive day-old beard against her sensitized skin. Then he reached her breasts again, his fascination with them as clear to her as to him. He nipped at her gently, then used his lips to sooth her heated skin, steadily, slowly, sensuously. She writhed beneath him, calling out his name, pleading for something, something more.

She was driving him crazy! Ken's movements were becoming erratic, frenzied, yet he couldn't stop himself. He warned himself to take it slow with her, but her uninhibited response was igniting an equal passion in him, egging him on to touch her without restraint. He slid his hands over her back, her arms, the sensitive spots on her stomach, then pressed warm kisses where his hands had been.

He kissed her thighs, and urged her legs apart as he continued his wanderings over her tender flesh.

Janet squirmed under the assault. These feelings were so new, so erotic, she didn't know how to respond; rather, how *not* to respond. So she allowed her feelings to take her along on this wild, roller-coaster ride.

He touched her everywhere, except for that one spot where she ached, craved for him to touch. She lifted her hips upward in a wordless plea for him to alleviate the throbbing need. She wanted him so badly, wanted to feel all of him, inside her, filling her, erasing the insistent yearning for ultimate completion.

Ken knew what she wanted and felt it as strongly as she did. He sat up into a kneeling position between her legs. His briefs barely contained his arousal, which strained at the material to be free. He put his hands high on her thighs, one on each side, and gently rubbed the soft mound of butter-colored curls with his thumbs as he stared down into her love-glazed eyes. His own mirrored her passion.

"What is it? What do you want?"

"You," she answered. "All of you."

In an instant he'd removed his briefs and flung them across the room. He knelt above her in all his naked glory, and she drank in the sight of him, proud and strong in his arousal. She had never viewed a man in this unabashed state before and it excited her beyond measure. A small worry ricocheted through her brain that perhaps she couldn't please him, but then Ken lowered his body down onto hers, and as the warm mat of chest hair touched her breasts, her mind went blank to all but sensation.

He kissed her, his entire weight on her as he lost himself in her softness. No woman had ever made him float on air this way. He lifted her legs and probed ever so gently until he felt her stiffen. It took him a moment to understand why, and when he did, he stopped cold. His heart began to sound in his chest as he raised his head to look at her.

"Janet?"

The incredulous look on his face said it all. "No, Ken. Please, oh, please don't stop! I want you to...I want you."

He began to shake his head, but she reached up and brought his lips to hers. She put her heart into that kiss, all the longing, all the loneliness, all the love of her life packed into a desperate plea for him to stay. She was so close, so near to having it all. She arched her hips upward, urging him on, squirming against him to drive away any doubts he might have.

With a groan Ken plunged into her, breaking the way through, once and for all time. Making love with Janet was a heady experience for him; he only hoped he wasn't hurting her. He wanted only to pleasure her, please her in every way, as she was pleasing him. And she was. The things that were happening to his body were so provocative, so erotic, that he could barely control his movements. She was perfect—and his. He kissed her again as he moved within her—kissed her neck, her ear, her throat—staking his claim; now and forever.

Janet was poised on a plateau she knew existed but had only dreamed of. She felt the power of his body fill her with a completeness that defied description. There was a building, growing force inside that wouldn't let her rest as she kept pace with him. It gradually expanded, slowly at first; then all of a sudden it became a sensation so incredible, so gripping and intense, she stiffened in fear of it. Ken felt her reaction and urged her on.

"Go with it, Janet. Don't hold back," he said. "Don't stop...let it take you..."

His persuasive coaxing and calming words helped her to relax as the feeling blossomed into a blinding eruption within as spasm after spasm rocked her body. She bit down onto his shoulder and groaned, mouth opened into his damp skin, and all the while he continued to thrust into her, rocking with her, absorbing the impact.

Ken's control was crumbling. He wanted this to go on forever, but his body wouldn't cooperate. The strength of her climax brought him to the brink of his own, and he felt himself falling, his mind failing to hold back his body as he, too, reached his ultimate goal.

And then it was over.

Ken raised himself onto his elbows to take some of his weight from her small frame. Her eyes were closed, and if not for the vibrant, pulsing vein in her neck, he would have thought she was sleeping. He watched her in wonder. Who was this woman? His wife, yes, but who else? She was untouched, yet had been married to J.D. for eight years. She had agreed to this marriage of convenience for the money and security, yet had responded to him here tonight in such a free, passionate way it took his breath away.

Janet opened her eyes to find Ken's quizzical gaze. She smiled, in too good a mood to let it bother her. She knew his confusion, and in a way relished it. She was so very happy right this minute that nothing, no one could ruin it. Not even the mighty Kenneth Gilbert Radnor.

"I bet you have a million questions," she said, laughing.

"You win the bet."

Suddenly she yawned. The overall exertion of making love had depleted the last vestiges of energy. She was totally drained and absolutely sleepy.

"Can we talk about this in the morning?"

Ken, on the other hand, was wide-awake now and wanted to know all there was to know about this woman to whom he was still joined in more ways than one.

"I won't be here in the morning, remember? I have to leave for the coast."

"Umm, yes. I do remember something like that." She shut her eyes as she spoke.

Ken moved from her and cradled her head in the nook of his arm and shoulder.

"Janet, we have to talk."

"Mmm...?"

"I said, we have to talk."

She turned on her side and snuggled more securely into his body's warmth.

"That was incredible, wasn't it?" she murmured.

He chuckled at her childish question, and raised her chin to look at him. She peered through half-closed lids.

"Yes, it was."

She returned his smile, a dreamy, faraway look on her beautiful face. She expelled a contented sigh as Ken brought the comforter up and covered both of them. He set his wrist alarm, then turned off the bedside lamp.

His need for talk was overruled by her need for sleep. It would have to wait. He settled his body around hers for the night. He felt happy, content and warm from the inside out. He had to admit that their lovemaking had been something very beautiful, special, a rare happening for the first time, if ever at all, between two people.

He kissed the top of her head and smiled to himself as he whispered into the darkness, "Definitely incredible."

Ken yawned. To say he was overtired would be a vast understatement. But his mind was on overload, running fast and furious, past exhaustion, somewhere on its way to euphoria. Somehow that trip to the coast tomorrow wasn't as welcome as before. He wondered how he would ever get through the day, not only physically because of lack of sleep, but mentally, trying to blot out the happenings of this evening and concentrate on business.

He pinched the bridge of his nose and shut his burning eyes, begging sleep to take him. Wouldn't it be great if Brian had it all wrapped up himself? He smiled at the thought and snuggled deeper down, closer to the warm body beside him.

Wouldn't it be great if he didn't have to go at all?

Five

―――

It was almost eight o'clock, Pacific time when Ken crawled into the suite at the Hyatt in San Francisco that he and Brian were sharing. He was absolutely wiped out, but before he succumbed to the welcome oblivion of sleep, he knew he had to speak to Janet, even if only for a minute. There hadn't been any time during the day to call. He'd always been surrounded by people, and what he had to say couldn't be said with an audience. She'd been on his mind constantly, lurking just shy of his consciousness, yet close enough to make him forget his train of thought. He'd lost count of how many times he'd asked "What was that?" or requested one of the men at the meeting to repeat himself. Brian had jokingly informed everyone that Ken's preoccupation was a result of his day-old marriage. His reputation as an astute businessman was still intact, although he had felt like a fool in front of men he respected as they'd good-naturedly chided him for leaving his bridal bed rather abruptly.

And *that* was the problem. Because there was nowhere on earth he would rather be right now than back in bed with Janet, naked and making love with her. There were so many things he wanted to show her, teach her. It was a heady experience, this virgin business. The possibilities were endless. The ideas tumbling inside his head fascinated him, as much as they excited him. He wanted to talk with her, be with her, hold her hand, touch her body, make love with her until he was completely drained. He wanted to sleep with her all night, holding her in his arms until dawn crept quietly into the room to wake them. And then he wanted to start all over again.

But he more than anyone understood the impossibility of doing any of these things. He had to control himself beyond any amount of control he'd ever exerted before. He had no idea how he was going to accomplish this feat, however, because even the thought of calling her on the phone was arousing him. What the hell was he going to do when they were actually together?

Ken reached for the phone. He took a deep breath and closed his tired eyes, pinching the bridge of his nose with his thumb and index finger to alleviate the burning sensation, as he listened to the phone ring. He prepared himself for the sound of her voice. *Oh, God,* he prayed, *why would you give me a woman I want more than anything else in the world, only to make her the one woman in the world I can't have?* It all seemed so unfair.

"Hello?"

"Edmund? It's Ken—"

"Kenneth! I expected to hear from you earlier."

"Yeah, well, it's a long story. I just got in. Uh, how's everything?"

"Fine, fine. How did the meeting go? Is Brian on his way home?"

"The meeting went better than expected, and yes, Brian's catching the red-eye later. He's going out on the town with a few people first."

"That's just like him. When I need to know specifics, he's off barhopping!"

"Edmund, please, don't start. I've had a long day and it's getting longer by the minute."

"Well, before you hang up, Doug Carmichael left a message with Eleanor at the wedding yesterday for you to call him."

"What about?"

"I've no idea. But we need to find out what he knows."

Ken sighed deeply, in no condition mentally to deal with the thought of Carmichael. "Okay, I'll call him in the morning. Do me a favor, will you, Ed? Get Janet for me? I need to speak to her."

Edmund hesitated for a moment. "She's not available right now."

"Where is she?"

"She's gone to bed. Said something about a headache at dinner and disappeared. She's probably asleep by now."

"Edmund, it's only eleven o'clock there. Go have someone get her. I'm sure she'll take my call."

"Kenneth, she, well, she specifically asked that she not be disturbed for any reason."

"Is something wrong?"

"No, no. I don't think so. She did get some telegrams today regarding the marriage, and seemed rather upset about her stepson, but I don't think it's anything serious."

"Then get her, Edmund."

"Very well."

Ken shut his burning eyes as he waited for what seemed like an eternity. He knew Edmund was curious as hell about what was going on between him and Janet; he could hear it in his voice. But how could he possibly explain to Edmund what he didn't understand himself?

"Kenneth?"

"Yes, Edmund, I'm still here. Where's Janet?"

"She says she doesn't want to speak to you."

"She *what*?"

"She says she's busy."

"Busy!" Ken was furious. Too busy to talk to him?

"Yes, well, that's what she said. Maybe she's in the middle of something. Shall I give her a message?"

"Yeah, you can tell her... No, forget it. I'll tell her myself when I see her. Whenever that may be."

Ken slammed down the receiver. Busy! What could be more important to her than talking to him? Especially after what they'd shared last night.

But perhaps they hadn't shared anything. Maybe it was only an experiment on her part, while to him it had been...making love, truly making love. He lay back on the bed and stared at the ceiling. He wished he knew what was going on in her mind. He wished he were there with her now to ask her. He wished he were there now to hold her, caress her. He closed his eyes and gave in to the lure of sleep.

He wished a lot of things.

He could have called.

It was almost midnight when Janet climbed into bed. The sheets were freshly laundered and cold to the touch. Just like her heart. He could have made *some* effort during the day or night to at least pick up the phone to see if she was alive or dead, or how she'd fared her first day in his home. It would have been common courtesy one would extend to any guest, let alone one's spouse.

The tears were swimming in her eyes for the fiftieth time that day, and she fought them back. Didn't he care at all? Hadn't it meant anything to him? God, how could what meant so much to her be so insignificant to him? Was that truly the way men were? Heartless, with all their feelings below the belt? She turned her face into the pillow and the tears spilled out, soaking through the fresh pillowcase. She told herself she wouldn't cry anymore, especially after she'd gone up to her rooms when dinner was over. *He'll call now,* she told herself at seven o'clock, at eight, at nine. Even when she heard the phone ring at eleven, her heart jumped. Surely that was him. He'd had a long, hard day and only now was able to get to a phone.

But no one came for her. She had to face the fact that he didn't care about her as a person. She was a business deal, fifteen percent of Radnor Corporation and nothing more. So, great, he'd gotten a little lucky last night. Who could blame him? She hadn't exactly fought him off with a stick, had she? What red-blooded male would pass up a willing female? "Willing" was an understatement! She covered her face with her hands as she relived how she'd behaved the night before. She'd been all over him, for pete's sake! No wonder he didn't call. He was probably totally turned off by the love-starved virgin who practically had to force him to have sex with her. How mortifying! Lord, she hoped he *never* returned from this business trip.

Well, she had to grow up sometime, she told herself. This was the real world, not J.D.'s dollhouse. She leaned over and pulled a tissue from the box, resolutely wiping her eyes, trying to force herself to think of something else.

She thought about her first dinner in the Radnor household. Always-elegant Eleanor sat at one end of the table with the ever-stern Edmund opposite her. The food, of course, was superbly prepared and delicious. The children, young Gil and Laura, were charming and well behaved. Their private school education showed itself in their impeccable table manners and speech. Janet couldn't have been more uncomfortable if she'd tried.

The only saving grace was when Gil dropped his napkin and he and Laura disappeared together under the table to retrieve it. The giggles were quickly suppressed by Edmund, but it did Janet's heart good to see the child in them surface. It reminded her of so many dinners spent with Peter when he was a little boy. They would joke and laugh and talk about the day's happenings. He would sometimes bring a toy to the table, and the two of them would sneak playing cars or another silly game under the table. She was just as much a child as he back then, and he was her heart's joy.

But Peter was no longer a little boy. If anything could, there was a thought to get her mind off Ken, pronto. At least a dozen telegrams had arrived for her today, all congratulating her on her marriage. Even Katherine had sent a wedding gift and a note wishing her happiness. Yet the one person who meant the most to her in the entire world never even acknowledged the event. It hurt. Peter didn't know that the marriage was meaningless. He could have been happy for her, as she'd been for him so many times over the years as he was growing up. She'd called Carlton that afternoon, but once again Peter refused to talk to her. She had to find a way to make amends with him. Paul had warned her he would react this way, but she still felt justified in not telling Peter the truth about their finances. She had to straighten out her problem with Peter before it festered into something beyond her control.

She'd made arrangements with Mr. Sagen to visit the school the day after tomorrow. She would have to force the issue, even if it meant telling Peter the truth. It wouldn't matter now; the damage was done—the wedding was over and the business arrangement in place. Peter would see that there would be no reason to be noble any longer. She realized that he had a right to be hurt and angry, but she had to find a way to convince him that she'd meant well, that she'd only been thinking of him and what was best for him. He would see her point and come around. He had to. He was the only reason she'd agreed to this insane proposition, and because of how she'd handled it, she was alone, without even Peter's love.

She snuggled down under the comforter that only last night covered two. Confusion and mixed emotions swirled in her head as she tried, without success, to sleep.

What had she done?

The moan woke him up. Ken paused to determine the source of the sound and was surprised to discover it was himself.

This time he groaned. The dream had been so real. Janet had been lying beneath him, whispering sweet words of encouragement in his ear, exciting him beyond the point of reason. He sat up and swung his legs over the edge of the bed, rubbing his eyes with the heels of his hands. Checking his watch, he saw how late it was. The wrist alarm hadn't gone off, or perhaps he'd never set it; he couldn't remember.

Standing, he glanced down and took note of his physical condition. This *had* to stop. What he needed was a cold, very cold shower. But more than that, he needed to get this woman out of his mind. An idea came to him as the first icy spray hit his face and body, shocking his nerve endings while doing an equally thorough job of diminishing his ardor. As goose pimples collected on his skin, he remembered he had to call Carmichael—and if that didn't get his mind off Janet, nothing would.

Douglas Carmichael. They'd been friendly enemies for so many years he refused to count them. When had it all started? In high school? Or was it that day at the country club? Ken remembered it all too clearly. It was one of those days that burned itself into the mind and would not, could not, go away no matter how hard one tried. To this day, Ken's face still burned with shame when he thought of it. He'd been only a kid then, feeling his oats—a bit selfish, a lot self-centered—and trying to impress a girl. He didn't remember the girl's name anymore, but that wasn't important. What was important was that he'd used his name, his money, his polish and his adolescent snobbery to put someone down, to keep him in his place, to just plain show off. That day returned to haunt him as if it were yesterday, and he purposely replayed the incident in his mind....

It had been summer and he'd been at the country club. Doug Carmichael had worked there. Coming from a poor, blue-collar family, Doug had had a fierce desire to better himself, a fact that had been obvious to all who met him. Ken's father had given Doug a job as his caddy, and on slow golf days, he would substitute at the snack bar.

It had been on one of those days that Ken had come up from the pool with some friends. He'd seen Doug at school and had even talked to him once or twice, but to say they were friends would have been an exaggeration. Doug had always been big, well over six feet even at that time, and he'd towered over the not-yet-fully-grown Ken. Ken's father had always spoken highly of Doug, praising his abilities and work ethic. That, too, had annoyed Ken no end, as he was always striving to please the old man.

His father wouldn't have been pleased with him that day. The group of kids had had the snack bar to themselves and they'd seated themselves at a table by the far end. Doug had glanced their way every so often, but had continued to clean off the countertop, paying no particular attention to the loud chatter of the group. It had irritated Ken that Doug was not more solicitous. After all, if it hadn't been for his father, the guy wouldn't have even had a job. The more he'd thought about his feelings for the big red-headed boy, the more obnoxious he'd become.

"Hey, you, boy!" Ken had shouted at Doug.

He remembered how Doug had stopped cold for a moment, then resumed his cleaning, only more slowly, in a more controlled manner this time. It had irked Ken to witness that control.

"Hey! Answer me! Can't you hear?"

Doug never looked up from his task. "I can hear you, Radnor, and so can half the club."

Ken strode over to the snack bar. "*Mr.* Radnor to you, Carmichael. Didn't your parents ever teach you how to speak to your betters?" Then Ken had turned around and smiled at his giggling audience.

Doug's already-ruddy complexion became even redder, if that was possible, but once again he kept his cool, which infuriated Ken all the more.

"What is it you want?" Doug had asked.

"Some Cokes. With lots of ice. Bring them over to the table. And make it snappy." Ken had knocked twice on the wooden counter to emphasize his order, then swaggered back to his group.

Soon after, Doug had carried a tray with four Cokes and had placed one in front of each person. As he'd turned to go, Ken deliberately had hit his drink with his elbow and the contents of the plastic cup had splattered all over the table and the floor. Doug had had fire in his eyes, and Ken remembered being frightened for a fleeting moment, until the prospect of a potential fight sent the adrenaline pumping through his teenage veins, and he'd thrown caution to the wind.

"Clean it up," he'd ordered with a glint in his eye and a smirk on his lips. Ken had watched the bigger boy fight a battle within himself. Doug was bigger and stronger by far, but Ken couldn't stop himself as he'd goaded him further.

"Don't forget who got you this job, Carmichael."

The threat hadn't been at all subtle and had hit its mark—shaking enough sense into Doug that he backed off. He'd returned with a new Coke and some towels to clean up the mess, but the hatred and contempt on his face were etched on Ken's memory, even after all these years. Ken wondered if Doug remembered that day as clearly as he did.

Ken turned off the water and toweled himself dry, rubbing a bit harder than necessary. It had been an awful thing to do; he'd known it then, as he knew it now. He'd discovered a feeling of power that day, he remembered, but the power had left a bitter taste in his mouth afterward. With that empty victory he'd learned an important lesson, one he'd never forgotten.

But at what price? For what perhaps could have been a friendship between two bright boys became instead a lifelong battle royal of competitiveness and one-upmanship that Ken couldn't change to this day. He'd never said he was sorry for what he'd done. He certainly felt sorry, but the opportunity had never presented itself. And so the wound had grown and festered as the enemy himself had grown—older, more successful, more powerful than anyone would have imagined that summer day long ago.

Carmichael Industries was a conglomerate that housed various companies, dwarfing Radnor Corporation by comparison. Yet Doug had never moved out of town. He'd stayed to watch, to plan and, to Ken's mind, to gloat. He was always after whatever the Radnors wanted, and he was ruthless in attaining his goals. Ken winced as he recalled the time Carmichael had outbid his father on a particularly involved deal that was supposed to be top secret. Gil Radnor had died soon after that, and Ken was convinced the loss to Carmichael had triggered his father's heart attack. He could forgive and forget many things, but not that, particularly because of all the help his father had given Doug over the years. It seemed especially cruel that Doug would stab Gil Radnor in the back like that. More than once Ken had wondered if that was Doug's way of getting back at him. It was a guilt he carried that no one, save possibly Doug, knew.

So Carmichael became Ken's nemesis; and the worst part of all was that Ken had brought it all on himself.

Ken finished dressing and placed the call. He was put through immediately, as was the custom whenever he and Doug phoned each other. There was an unwritten rule of never letting the other wait too long, even if one of them had to leave a meeting to take the call. It was almost as if they enjoyed the conflict.

"Kenneth! And how is the bridegroom this fine day? You surprised all of us. She *is* still around, isn't she?"

The zing hit its mark as the long-lost memory of his first wife's desertion came to mind. Ken chose to ignore the barb. He, too, had learned control over the years.

"What do you want, Carmichael? Edmund told me you said you *had* to speak to me. What about?"

Doug sighed audibly. "You never loosen up, do you, Kenneth? I guess that's what comes of taking lessons from Edmund for so long."

Ken gritted his teeth and fought the urge to hang up. "The point, Carmichael. Get to the point."

"Okay, the point. I've made no secret of the fact that I want a seat on your board of directors."

"Tell me something I don't know."

"What you don't know, Ken, is that I have a deal for you—a deal that will inject a huge amount of much-needed capital into your corpor—"

"We don't need—"

"Yes, you do. I talked to Paul Bradly at your wedding yesterday. That man was a virtual fountain of information." Doug paused for effect. "I know the whole story."

Ken cursed under his breath and made a mental note to call Paul and ask him what in hell he thought he was doing.

"That doesn't change anything, and you know it. The stock is in the family now that Janet and I are married. So just forget whatever you thought you heard," Ken said, ready to hang up.

"For once in your life, listen to me. Be reasonable. You need the money—I have it. I'm also willing to include Bradford, Ltd. in the deal."

"The company you stole out from under my father?"

"I could never 'steal' anything from Gil Radnor and you know it. That man was like a father to me—he gave me my start. I respected him, consulted with him—"

"Killed him. Spare me the hearts and flowers, Carmichael. I'm not interested in doing business with you. Not now. Not ever."

"You're wrong about your father and me. If you'd just give me an hour with an open mind, I can explain everything."

"Edmund would never agree to even speak to you."

"I'm not asking Edmund. I'm asking you."

Ken expelled a breath of frustration. "Let me make this real clear and simple—*I'm* not interested. Ed's not interested and even Brian's not interested. Got it?"

"How about your wife?" Doug asked, his voice low, deep, almost threatening.

Ken stopped for a moment, then answered slowly, "In particular, my wife's not interested."

"We'll see about that."

"Keep away from her, Douglas."

"You leave me no choice. You won't speak to me. Maybe the lady would be more receptive to a cash settlement."

"She won't talk to you. I've already filled her in on you and your interest in her only for the stock."

Doug chuckled. "Who says I'm only interested in her stock?"

Ken could almost see the Cheshire grin through the telephone. He warned himself not to rise to the bait, but where Janet was concerned, his emotions weren't his own. His silence was answer enough for Doug.

"Worried, Kenneth? Could it be I've found your Achilles' heel after all these years? Hmm . . . interesting . . . I'll have to think about this." Doug paused and lowered his voice again. "You do the same."

The click of the receiver sounded like an explosion in Ken's ear. Could Doug convince Janet to sell? Ken had to admit the possibility was there, especially if her recent attitude toward him was any indication of her true feelings. It was up to him to see it didn't happen.

He slowly hung up the phone. He had to cut this trip short and get home. He had work to do.

He had to woo his wife.

Six

All of a sudden, he was there. As she made the turn around the second landing of the stairway, suitcase in hand, she almost ran smack into him. Janet had rehearsed every imaginable meeting, but the reality was startling nonetheless. The beating of her heart accelerated to an alarming rate as she faced him, mouth open, mind void of a single thing to say, clever or otherwise.

"H-hello!" she managed to spit out, her hand on her heart, desperately trying to calm the loud thumping so that he wouldn't hear.

If Janet had had the presence of mind to notice, she would have clearly seen that Ken's discomfit was as great, if not greater, than her own. He'd slipped into the house unnoticed, hoping to make his way to Brian's rooms before anyone came down to dinner. He wanted to shower, shave and refresh himself after his exhausting trip. He'd hoped to be ready to do battle with Janet, if necessary, at the dinner table, where there would be people around to act as a buffer.

But running into her like this scrambled all his plans. Once again he was reduced to acting like a schoolboy, uncertain about what he should say, how he should act. He knew what he *wanted* to do. He wanted to take her into his arms and just hold her, breathing in her scent, feeling her warmth. He was unprepared for the ferocity of the urge, and gripped the banister to stop himself from reaching out to her.

"Hi." He expelled the word on a breath.

She made note of his agitation, but refused to dwell on it at the moment. She was too busy examining him. He looked tired and a bit rumpled, as if he'd spent more than one day in those clothes. That in itself should have given her cause for reflection; Ken was usually impeccably groomed. But it was the look in his eyes that affected her most of all. They were emotionless. She could read nothing, except perhaps a touch of caution. Of what was he wary? Certainly not her!

"I didn't expect you back until the end of the week," she said. She'd promised herself she wouldn't mention the fact that he hadn't called.

"Things moved more quickly than planned. The meetings ran longer with each client, so we were able to complete our business sooner." Why was he telling her any of this? He didn't owe her any explanations! He'd rushed through those meetings so that he could be home with her. But, then, she would have known his intentions if she'd accepted his call!

"You must have been *very* busy," she said.

"As busy as you, I suppose."

"What's that supposed to mean?"

Ken was more than annoyed. He certainly didn't need her third degree as he stood there on the steps after the grueling two days he'd just had! He did have to hand it to her, though. She had a lot of nerve bringing up the subject in the first place. But he would be damned if he was going to be put on the defensive!

"You figure it out," he said. He brushed past ner on the stairs, and he noticed the suitcase.

"Going somewhere?"

"Yes. I'm on my way up to see Peter."

Ken frowned. "Can you wait until tomorrow to leave?"

Janet shook her head. "No. I've already made arrangements to see him first thing in the morning. I'm driving up tonight and staying over."

"I see. Do you need to leave right this minute?"

"Ken, it's a three-hour drive. I'd like to get started. Besides, I don't see what difference it makes to you when I leave."

"I'd like to go with you," he said.

She paused; she hadn't expected that. "Why?"

"Why not?" he answered. "Peter and I have yet to meet each other. Wouldn't he think it odd if you left your new husband at home?"

Janet hadn't even considered the possibility at all. Somehow she'd never put Peter and Ken together in her mind. They were two separate and distinct entities in her life, connected only through her—and the stock.

"I suppose," she said. "But it really isn't necessary for you to come along. Peter and I need to discuss some things that have nothing to do with our marriage. I know how tired you must be—"

"I want to come."

"Well, if that's the case, I guess I could wait awhile, if you insist."

"I insist," Ken said. "I'll meet you in the study in a few minutes."

She nodded and he disappeared from view. Janet shut her eyes and gritted her teeth. This was going to complicate everything. Since the first moment she'd seen him walk into the study on their wedding day, he'd required an inordinate amount of her attention. She'd planned to spend the drive up concentrating on Peter, on what she would say, how she would handle him. Now she wouldn't be able to do that. She should have been more assertive. Yet part of her warmed to the idea of having Ken with her. He seemed genuinely to want to come along. Why? Did he truly want to be involved in her life? The idea both seduced and frightened her.

Janet turned and continued down the stairs. She put her suitcase down in the hallway and made her way into the study. As she waited for Ken's return, she paced the room. In less than half an hour, the door opened and he walked into the room, casually dressed and freshly showered. The well-worn jeans rode low on his hips, and the forest-green cable-knit sweater went well with his dark coloring. She realized she'd never seen him wearing anything other than a suit—except for when he hadn't been wearing anything at all....

"Ready?" he asked.

"Yes," she said, brushing past him on her way out the door.

Ken stopped her with a hand on her arm. She looked up at him. His eyes were black as midnight and as deliberately penetrating as ever. What did he want from her?

"Truce?" he said softly. He could tell she was uptight and he didn't want to fight with her.

"No. I want to know what you meant on the stairs before."

"Let's not discuss it now."

"When will we discuss it, Ken? Tonight? Tomorrow? Or maybe after your next urgent business trip!"

"Don't get on your high horse with me, Janet. *I'm* not the one who's been busy!"

Janet shook her head slightly as if to clear it. "I thought you said you were very busy during your trip."

"Couldn't you tell I was being sarcastic? You were the one too busy to take my call!"

"What call? You called me?" Her heart leaped and rolled over in her chest.

"Of course I called you! Did you think I wouldn't? I called you last night. You were too busy to talk to me—"

"No—"

"Edmund said—"

"No—"

"Edmund never told you? Never called you to the phone? Didn't tell you I called at all?"

Janet shook her head to each of his questions. Ken muttered a threatening obscenity and swiftly pulled her into his arms.

"I'll kill him—I swear it! With my bare hands I'll kill him!"

Janet's face was buried in his chest. She mumbled without moving. "Then you *did* call?"

Her voice was small, meek, and until that moment he hadn't realized how vulnerable she truly was.

"Yes. It was late in the day, but I had to speak to you. I was so wound up..."

He lifted her face, cradling it with both hands as he stared deeply into her striking blue eyes.

"How could you think I wouldn't? Especially after our night together? I couldn't get you out of my mind all the next day, or since, for that matter!"

Janet felt the joy burst through her like an overfilled water balloon, its liquid warmth seeping down through to her limbs, making her too weak to stand. She wrapped her arms around his waist for support, as well as to touch him, feel his strength. He was home, and he wanted her!

"Janet."

His voice was as soft as the breath that caressed her face. His lips touched hers gently before his opened mouth covered hers in a deep, soul-searching kiss. All thought left her mind as she sagged into him. He wrapped his arms around her body, pulling her closer against him, the contact total, complete. His tongue warmed the hidden corners of her mouth, conquering the territory, making it his own. She joined him in loving battle as her senses reeled. She lifted her hands to his shoulders, his neck. Wanting to touch him, feel him, she ran her hands over his face, her fingers gliding lightly and feather soft. The heat that emanated from his skin was alarming as well as gratifying.

He released her lips and kissed her neck, sending convulsive shivers through her body. She pushed herself into him, rubbing provocatively against him. Ken leaned against the back of the sofa for support and held her to him for a moment before looking down at her. His hair was tousled, and a look of chagrin adorned his face.

"I guess this is neither the time nor the place."

"I guess not," Janet agreed.

She looked at him in embarrassment. He had a smudge of her lipstick at the corner of his mouth and she lifted her thumb to wipe it away. Once again she'd thrown herself at him like a love-starved spinster. What must he think of her?

Janet stepped away from him to straighten her clothes. He put out his hand, and she readily placed hers in it. He brought the hand to his lips and gently kissed the palm.

She wanted him to kiss her again, and perhaps for that reason alone, she pulled her hand away. "It's getting late. We'd better leave."

Ken smiled, a slow, understanding smile. She needed to take control. He needed to let her. Things were moving too quickly between them. His initial attraction the day of the wedding had ignited into anger and resentment. But then they'd made love, and everything had changed. Too much, too soon. He needed to get to know her and she, him, before things went any further. The rational part of him accepted this truth; the problem was in convincing the very physical part of himself, which of late had developed a rather stubborn mind of its own.

He ushered her out of the study and out of the house. They waited in silence as a servant brought a shiny silver Porsche to the circular drive and loaded their bags into the trunk. Ken opened the passenger door and helped her in.

"Your car?" she asked.

"My passion," he said with a grin.

She returned his devilish smile and strapped herself in while she waited for him to seat himself.

Janet gave him directions and then concentrated on the road for a few minutes as they pulled away from the house. She turned to watch him and noticed his jaw, clenched and working overtime.

"I hope that scowl isn't for me," she said.

"What?" He gave her a quick glance. "Oh. No. Edmund."

"Why would he do such a thing, Ken? I don't understand it."

"Don't you? It's pretty clear to me. He's protecting his investment. Namely our marriage—or should I say, our annulment?"

"Oh. I see."

"Yes. Well, it's about time Edmund learned how to mind his own business."

"But Ken..." Janet hesitated, grateful for the darkness so that he couldn't see her cheeks turning pink. "There can no longer *honestly be* an annulment, can there?"

Ken stopped at a red light and looked at her. "No, Janet, I *honestly* don't believe there can be."

She heard the chuckle in his voice and turned away, pretending to observe the scenery out of the passenger window. She felt like such a child around him sometimes. She leaned back against the headrest and sighed, dispelling the thought. It was very dark now and this portion of the thruway didn't have any lights. Traffic was light and only an occasional headlight illuminated the area. The night was brisk, but she refused his offer of heat. She needed the cool air to keep her alert. She had a lot of thinking to do.

Ken noted her discomfort and chided himself. He reminded himself how inexperienced she was in some ways, and how quickly she became embarrassed when he teased. She seemed lost in thought, and he wished he could peek over the rim of her mind and discover her true feelings about the situation in which they found themselves.

"What are you thinking about?" he asked.

Janet sighed and moved her head from right to left without lifting it from the headrest.

"Peter."

"Problem?"

A mirthless laugh escaped her lips. "You could say that. He refuses to speak to me."

"Because of me?"

"No, because of me. I didn't tell him the truth about our financial situation. I didn't lie. I just didn't tell him at all."

"What did you tell him about our marriage?"

"I never mentioned the contract, so he doesn't know about the stock. He thinks we married for—"

"For love?"

Janet studied his profile. It was too dark to read his feelings, if indeed there were any to read.

"Yes."

"I see."

"Do you?" she asked. "He's very angry at me. And hurt. God, I hurt him so much, and that's the one thing in the world I promised myself I wouldn't do."

"You should have told him. How old is he? Fourteen?"

"Yes." She sighed. "And I know that now. I wanted to protect him. He's been through so much already in his short life. First the accident, and now his father's death. I just couldn't tell him about the money."

"If I'm any judge of teenage boys, I'd say he's feeling betrayed and abandoned right about now. You've got your work cut out for you tomorrow. Want some moral support when you meet him?"

"I'd love some. But I don't think your presence would help the situation, if you know what I mean. Thank you for offering, but I think I'd better handle this alone."

Ken nodded his acceptance of her decision. Part of him wanted to argue the point, but the other, less emotional side realized that this was something she had to do herself. She and Peter obviously had a special relationship. He was the stranger in the situation. It was funny how much that bothered him. Up until now, he never needed to feel part of anything except his business and his family.

"He's very special to you," Ken said.

"He's all I have."

"No other family?"

"No. My mother died when I was ten and I never knew my father. I had no other relatives, so I became a ward of the state and was placed in several foster homes." She smiled sadly. "Ten-year-old girls aren't very adoptable, unfortunately."

"You don't sound bitter."

"I'm not. My foster parents were all good people, and they tried their best, for the most part. I have no hidden horror stories. But my life didn't really start until I met Katherine, J.D.'s sister."

"Is that when you went to work for J.D.?"

"Yes. Katherine brought me to his home to care for Peter. He was only six at the time. The most confused, lonely, frightened little boy you've ever met. His mother was dead and his father locked himself away for hours at a time. It was pitiful." Janet sat up, turned in the seat toward Ken and continued, "But all that soon changed. Peter and I became fast friends. I was only eighteen at the time myself, and had all this love stored up inside. It was the perfect setting for me to blossom in."

"And then you married J.D."

"Yes." She sighed again. "Some people thought we were crazy. But if you think about it, it made sense. J.D. was the father, uncle, brother I never had. He was a strong-minded, stubborn man who took care of me. And I let him. I was so tired of taking care of myself, it was a relief to give myself over to someone else. He sent me to college and helped me get the job at the university. He gave me everything."

Ken slowed down and pulled the car off the road onto the shoulder. He cut the engine and turned toward her in the seat. Janet was just about to question him, when he took hold of her hand in both of his. A heavy silence filled the car as he stared down at the long slim fingers and toyed with them, deep in thought.

"No, Janet. He didn't give you everything." He looked up at her, still caressing her hand. His piercing gaze skimmed her face briefly before coming to rest on her eyes.

She smiled, and tightened her fingers around his. "No," she said softly, "not everything. You gave me a very special gift, and I thank you for that."

"I don't want your thanks. I want it to continue."

Janet pulled her hand away. "Oh, Ken, how can it? What happened between us the other night was beautiful, but it can't go on. We have a business arrangement, nothing more...."

"What if I said I wanted it to be more?"

"I don't know." She shook her head. "I don't know."

"Come here."

She was wary of his intentions, but complied, scooting over nearer to him. Ken leaned toward her, his face only inches away.

"I'm not any more certain about all this than you, Janet." He lifted a finger and lightly trailed it from her temple to her chin. "I was prepared to hate you for this. I didn't want to get married again." She began to speak, but he moved his finger to her lips to still her words. "Something's happened though. I'm feeling things I never have before. While I admit I don't understand it all, I know one thing for sure—I don't want it to stop." He brushed the finger back and forth across her lower lip. "Let it happen, Janet. Don't kill what's growing between us."

"I'm afraid," she whispered, her sapphire eyes shimmering in the darkness.

"So am I," he said. "I stopped looking a long time ago for that special 'something' people talk about. But I'd hate to be fool enough not to recognize it when it comes along."

"Do you really think we could—"

His lips replaced his finger and he rubbed them back and forth across her opened mouth. "Let's find out."

He kissed her, and a jolt of desire ricocheted around her insides, shaking her to the core. She ran her hands through the thickness of his hair as he moved so that she could rest her head on his shoulder. Cradling her tightly, he cupped the back of her head with one strong hand, gently massaging the muscles in her neck.

"I want you," he whispered.

Janet whimpered, a tiny, incoherent sound, and Ken brought his lips to hers, the kiss complete, thorough.

A tap on the windshield and the glare of a powerful flashlight broke them apart.

"You all right in there?" The state trooper's voice echoed through the closed window.

Ken released her and pressed the button to open the window.

"Yes, officer," he said. "We're fine."

"I saw the car pulled over. I thought you might need help."

"No, everything's okay."

The trooper flashed the light quickly throughout the car's interior before turning it off.

"Better get a move on, then. It's dangerous to park on the side like this."

"Sure thing," Ken said, and restarted the engine.

The trooper nodded and walked back to his car.

Ken turned toward an embarrassed Janet and laughed. "It's been a long time since I've been caught necking in a car."

"I've *never* been caught necking in a car!"

"I can see where parts of your education have been sorely lacking," he teased, and leaned over to kiss her nose. "We'll have to work on that."

"Ken..." she warned.

"I'll be good," he said as he checked the side and rear-view mirrors before pulling back onto the thruway.

Janet shifted closer to the door.

"Don't go away," he said.

She shook her head. "You confuse me too much. It's safer over here. Somehow I lose all self-control if I come within a foot of you!"

"Yeah?" He grinned, pleased with her pronouncement.

"Yeah."

"I like that."

"I wish I were as sure as you," she added more somberly.

Ken reached for her hand and gave it a short, tight squeeze.

"I won't push you, I promise," he said, the laughter gone from his voice. "Just promise me you'll think about what I said, okay?"

She caught the sincerity in his eyes before they returned to the road. "Okay," she promised.

His stomach growled loudly, and they both laughed. It was just the thing to lighten the mood.

"As you can tell, I haven't eaten anything all day. Do you mind if we stop on the way?"

"Not at all. I know a place about ten miles from here—an informal pub, if that's all right with you."

"That'll be fine."

They rode in companionable silence the remainder of the trip to the restaurant. A calm descended over Janet. It was good to spend time with Ken like this. The strength she'd sensed the day they'd met came through in the sound of his voice and the way he expressed his thoughts. She felt the invisible tug of his personality drawing her closer to him. It wasn't an unwanted feeling.

The restaurant wasn't particularly crowded and they were served quickly. She noted his exhaustion and offered to drive the rest of the way. He agreed, and soon after dinner and coffee they were on the road again. The caffeine didn't seem to help, because within minutes Ken was asleep in the passenger seat, leaving Janet slightly in awe of the powerful machine she was driving. It was fun and it made her feel as if she hadn't a care in the world. Maybe things would work out, after all.

She woke him when they pulled into the country bed-and-breakfast inn at which she'd made reservations for the night. They carried their own bags inside and registered. When they were shown to their room, Janet panicked at the sight of the double bed. She waited until the owner left before speaking her concerns.

"Ken, I ... think we should see about another room."

Ken was still groggy, but alert enough to know the reason for her discomfort.

He put down the bag in the middle of the floor and walked toward her. Taking her shoulders in both hands, he said, "I made you a promise during the drive up here. I meant it. I won't rush you, or force you to do anything you don't want to do. You know how I feel. You know what I want. But it's your decision if we ever make love again." He grinned sheepishly. "And anyway, I'm so out of it tonight, I don't think I could do you justice even if you allowed it. Let me sleep with you tonight, just sleep. Okay?"

She placed her hands on his and smiled. "Okay."

He nodded and moved away from her. He was undressed so quickly she didn't have time to protest. She did have time, however, to appreciate the sheer masculinity of his body. Left with only the slimmest of briefs, he strode over to the bed, pulled down the covers and climbed in. Within minutes he was asleep.

Janet lifted her bag and entered the bathroom. At least one of them would sleep tonight.

Seven

———

Janet was completely dressed and almost ready to leave when Ken opened his eyes for the first time the next morning. He watched as she applied her makeup, noticing her jerky movements and shaky hands. She was nervous, tense...and scared. It disturbed him to know he was at least partly responsible, and he searched his brain for something to say to ease her mind.

"Morning," he said as he pushed himself up to a sitting position.

"Hi," Janet answered, the brief smile disappearing as quickly as it had come. "I'm sorry if I woke you. I tried to be as quiet as possible. I need to get over to the school before Peter's first class begins."

"No, you didn't wake me, but you should have." He swung his legs out from under the covers and over the side of the bed. "Give me ten minutes and I'll drive you over."

Janet turned from the mirror. "You don't have to—"

"I want to," he said, cutting off her protest. "I'll stay out of the way. I just want to be there for you if you need me. Okay?"

She gave him a tight smile and nodded. "Okay."

He returned the nod and disappeared into the bathroom. Janet put down the lipstick and stared at the depression on his pillow and the rumpled sheets. It would be so easy for her to chuck it all and hop back into bed with Ken. She could lose herself in him, pretending that they were just another happy couple spending some time away in a quiet country inn. The thought was as tempting as it was cowardly, and she shook her head, banishing it from her mind. She stared at her reflection in the mirror, but the face that stared back was Peter's—resentful, angry and hurt. The pull of her duty to him was strong, stronger than even these new, uncharted emotions, and now duty called.

Satisfied with her handiwork, she touched up her makeup and walked toward the bathroom. Through the closed door, she could hear the shower running. She opened the door a crack and poked her head into the steam-filled room.

"Ken? I'll meet you downstairs, okay?"

It took him a heavy second to respond in the affirmative. He listened intently and heard the sounds of the door closing behind her as she left the room. He lifted his face to the spray of hot water and allowed it to engulf him. Thoughts ran through his mind much the way the rivulets of water streamed down his face.

As soon as he'd opened his eyes, it was obvious that the long, lingering kiss he'd dreamed about and the morning spent in bed were out of the question. This Janet was all business. He marveled at this chameleon quality of hers: her ability to go from soft and vulnerable to cool and professional in the blink of an eye. He turned off the faucets and stepped out onto the cold tile floor. While he acknowledged her need to do this alone, he also accepted his own need to be included. He was too attuned to his own emotions not to realize that this feeling, this *need*, was something different. Want and desire were familiar territory, but this was something totally new.

He wiped the condensation from the mirror with the towel and prepared to shave. He was unsure of the outcome of their relationship, but not altogether uncomfortable with how all this was affecting him. In many ways he welcomed the challenge, for he liked nothing better. He felt an excitement bubbling inside, as if something important were about to happen. The feeling was similar to the rush he experienced when a difficult deal was put to rest, yet better, more intense. He was a little in awe of it, wouldn't put a name on it, but definitely didn't want it to stop.

He grinned. Maybe he was falling in love.

Janet observed Peter as he entered the room and walked directly to the window, as far from her as humanly possible. His profile was visible to her as he concentrated his attention on the dreary autumn landscape. He hadn't even greeted her.

She'd left Ken with the headmaster, and for a fleeting moment wished he were there beside her for support, moral or otherwise.

She noted the differences in the boy the minute she saw him. His brown curly hair was longer, hanging over his collar and his usually warm brown eyes looked troubled. There was also a smattering of soft down whiskers visible on his chin and above his upper lip. He'd changed these past few months, but more so, he'd aged—not *grown* as so many boys were apt to do in giant spurts—but actually *aged*. His face held a sadness that seemed permanent, and it broke her heart to know that she'd brought about that look.

"Peter," she implored, "please look at me." Her voice was soft, coaxing.

Peter turned slowly, and his icy stare hit her with such force she felt the chill to her bones. The unrelenting stare and closed expression spoke volumes of how he felt about her.

"Are you by yourself?" he asked.

"Yes, of course."

"Where's your husband?"

Janet hesitated.

"Isn't this your honeymoon?" he sneered.

"Peter, please . . . let me explain."

"Explain what, Janet? Dad's been dead only two months, and you're married again. How long were you going out with your new husband before he died? Huh?"

"Peter! I never—"

"Do you know what the guys are saying about you? Do you?" Peter asked, his voice cracking.

"It's not like that. We never met. Not until the day of the wedding. Please sit down and let me tell you how all this happened. Let me say what should have been said months ago. Please," she said again when he hadn't moved.

Peter's face was like stone, but she noticed his Adam's apple bobbing with emotion. He moved toward the couch and sat down.

Janet cleared her throat and tried, as best she could, to explain all that Paul Bradly had told her about their financial problems. She talked about the stock, about the deal she'd made with the Radnor family, about her marriage. She told him it would be temporary and soon, very soon, it would be just the two of them again.

"So you see, nothing's really changed, Peter. I haven't left you and started a new life. This is a business arrangement."

"Why didn't you tell me before? We could have worked it out. We always talked about everything together—you, Dad and me."

"I know. I'm sorry. It seemed so simple at the time, but now I see that I should have told you. I wanted to protect you—"

He stood up. "I'm not a baby, Janet! You could have told me what was going on. I can take care of myself!"

"Peter, please. You would have had to leave school. Don't you understand? I wouldn't have been able to afford to keep you here."

"I would've left school—gotten a job."

"Don't be ridiculous! You're fourteen years old. And you know how your father felt about this school."

Tears were filling his eyes as he tried, unsuccessfully, to keep his emotions under control.

"I know how my father felt about the house, too, Janet, and you sold that! You never asked me what *I* wanted. You're living with him now. You have a new family. You don't need me!"

As he strode past her toward the door, she grabbed his arm. "Don't say that, Peter. It's not true. You're my only family. I love you. Please listen to me."

The tears threatening to spill over, he shrugged free of her. "No!" he shouted. "Go back to him! I don't need you! I don't need anyone! Just leave me alone!" He stormed out the door, slamming it against the wall as he practically ran down the hall, almost knocking over the headmaster and Ken at the same time.

Ken quickly turned and entered the sitting room, finding Janet, as he knew he would, hunched over on the couch, crying her eyes out.

"What happened?"

Janet looked up, tears streaming down her face, and attempted to wipe her eyes with the backs of her hands. She rose and walked over to the table where her purse was and extracted a tissue to wipe her eyes.

"He's so unforgiving, Ken, so alone! I said all the wrong things. I can't get through to him. My explanations seemed so strong before I faced him, but even to my ears they were thin. Just imagine what they must have sounded like to him!" She blotted her face. "I thought I was doing the right thing, but he's not a little boy anymore and I don't know how to reach him."

Ken wrapped his arms around her. His compassion warred with his own resentment toward the boy. Janet loved Peter, and Peter had hurt her beyond measure, denying the love she offered so freely. He realized he was jealous, and chided himself for his selfishness, but what had just happened made his blood boil, and he knew he had to do something about it. "What now?" he asked.

Janet took a deep breath and looked up at him. She read the concern in his face.

"Do you mind if we go back to the inn for a while? I have a splitting headache."

"Of course," he said. "Let's go."

They met Mr. Sagen on the way out.

"Give him time, Mrs. Radnor. Boys this age are very volatile. You'll see. He'll come around."

She nodded and allowed Ken to guide her to the car.

They drove to the inn in silence, lost in their own thoughts. Once he'd settled Janet in the room, Ken made the excuse of having to make several business calls. He told her he would use the phone downstairs so as not to disturb her rest.

He did indeed have some business to attend to, but it had nothing to do with Radnor Corporation. In no time at all, he found himself back at Carlton, facing a startled Mr. Sagen.

"Mr. Radnor! Did you forget something?"

"In a way. I'd like to speak to Peter."

The headmaster peered around Ken, apparently in search of Janet. "Mrs. Radnor—"

"No. Just me."

"Follow me. He was quite upset when he returned to his room. I'll see if he'll speak to you. You can meet him in the same room, if that's all right."

"That'll be fine." Ken walked back to the small sitting room at the end of the hall and waited, unsure of what he would say, but determined to speak his mind.

What seemed like an eternity was in reality only a few minutes. Ken stopped pacing as soon as Peter appeared in the doorway. Mr. Sagen urged him forward and shut the door.

The two faced each other as if measuring up an opponent. Ken cleared his throat and approached Peter first, his hand outstretched in greeting.

"Hello, Peter. I'm Ken Radnor. We've never met, but your father and my father were good friends."

Peter's grip was firm, and Ken intuitively knew that the mere mention of J.D. was enough to get the boy's attention. He would make a good impression for his father's sake, even if it killed him.

"Yes," Peter said. "I know who you are. You're Janet's new husband. Did she send you?"

"No. As a matter of fact, she doesn't even know I'm here. I thought you and I might have a talk, get to know each other."

Peter looked him straight in the eye but didn't answer. Ken saw through the defiance to the frightened, nervous young man. Myriad adolescent memories surged forth as Ken empathized with him. Fourteen was a tough age for a boy. For anyone, he supposed.

"You hurt her very much today," Ken said softly.

Peter turned away. "Why don't you both just leave me alone. It's what you really want anyway."

"That's not true. Janet wants you with her. She was telling the truth about our marriage. It's a business deal, nothing more."

Peter looked back at him. "I don't believe you."

"It's true. Ask Paul Bradly. Everything she's done, she's done for you. She didn't plan this, but it was the best way out of a bad situation." He walked closer. "You can see that, can't you?"

"Why didn't she tell me? Why did she have to pretend everything was fine?"

"She didn't want to upset you any more than you already were. She thought the money—or I should say the lack of money—would be too much for you to take right after your father's death. She may have been wrong, but her heart was in the right place. Janet loves you."

"And what about you? Does she love you, too?"

The question took Ken by surprise and he arched his brows speculatively. "I don't know. I think it's a little soon for that, don't you?" Ken smiled.

"You like her," Peter said, "don't you?"

"Yes, I like her. Any objections?"

Peter studied him for a minute, then shrugged. "I don't care."

Ken almost laughed out loud at his pretended nonchalance, but controlled the urge.

"Peter, I know you're hurt. I know you've been through a lot these past years, been hurt by things beyond your control." Ken took a step closer. "But you can control what you're feeling right now about Janet. Give her the benefit of the doubt. Talk to her, tell her what you're feeling."

"You want me to forgive her, is that it? Forgive and forget, just like that," he said, snapping his fingers, then he rolled his eyes and stared at the ceiling. "It's not as easy as you make it sound."

"I'm not saying it's easy. I'm not even saying you're wrong. This whole affair was handled badly. It was poorly thought out on all our parts. It was a business deal, and unfortunately, business deals don't take feelings into consideration."

Ken walked over to stand directly in front of Peter. He was surprised to see that he was only slightly taller than the boy. Janet was right. Peter was well on his way to becoming his own man.

"What you need in your life right now is someone to hold on to, someone to take from and give to, someone to love. Janet is here for you. Don't throw that away. You may never find another like her."

Ken put a hand on Peter's shoulder and gave a gentle squeeze. He turned to go, not knowing what else to say, feeling he may already have done more damage than good by this impulsive act of returning to see Peter.

"You sound like you're talking about yourself more than me," Peter said.

Ken turned, startled by the boy's intuitiveness. He grinned. "Maybe I am."

Ken left the room, resisting the urge to look back to see Peter's reaction.

Ken didn't return to the inn right away. He drove around the countryside, rehashing his meeting with Peter over and over. He supposed he could have handled it better. Peter was just a kid, after all. Then again, other than Laura and Gil, he really had no experience in dealing with children. But he'd wanted to help Janet in any way he could. He'd wanted to protect his woman. He smiled to himself at the macho phrase, but the more he played with the idea, the more appealing it became. Janet, his woman. He loved the sound of it.

How much he'd really helped her was debatable, though. Peter was as unresponsive with him as he'd been with her. Ken thought a man-to-man talk would be less emotional, yet Peter had stubbornly refused to relent. At this point Ken just hoped to hell he hadn't made the situation worse.

He finally returned to the inn near lunchtime and decided to make those phone calls he'd used as an excuse earlier. He avoided calling Edmund because he still hadn't gotten over his anger enough even to talk to his brother. When he was through, he glanced at his watch and wondered if Janet was ready for lunch.

He knew he should go see how she was doing. He based his reluctance on the fact that he couldn't handle her crying anymore. But if the truth be told, it was his own guilt that held him back. What if his rash action completely alienated Peter? Should he tell her what he'd done? She had a right to know, of course, but he couldn't exactly figure out how to explain to her the urgent need for action he'd experienced this morning. Somehow he didn't think his "protect my woman" reason would go over too well!

He sighed, squared his shoulders and stood. *Time to face the music, Kenneth,* he commanded himself. He clenched his jaw and prepared to face a puffy-eyed, sniffling, sad-faced Janet as he climbed the stairway and unlocked the door to their room.

She was puffy eyed, and there was a huge pile of crumpled tissues on the floor, but there was definitely no sad face. Janet was sitting Indian-style in the middle of the bed, the phone in her lap and the biggest, widest, toothiest smile he'd seen to date on her face.

"Ken!" She jumped off the bed and practically flung herself into his arms.

He reacted immediately and brought her body flush against his own. He closed his eyes to savor the feeling.

Janet pulled back. "He called! Ken, he actually called me back. I can't believe it!"

"Peter?"

"Yes! He must have had a change of heart. I don't know. I don't care!"

Ken watched her dance around the room and returned her smile. *So the kid called. Fancy that.*

"What did he say?"

"He wants to talk to me. We're going to have lunch together. I think he may have even apologized. I was so excited, I don't even remember! He seemed so...so, oh, I don't know...so like the old Peter, my Peter. Before this wretched mess ever began."

Janet was so jubilant she failed to notice Ken's reaction to her words. Was being his wife so "wretched"? It amazed him that such a simple comment could wound so deeply.

"I'm meeting him at one o'clock. Do you want to come along? It would be a great time for you to meet him."

"No," Ken said cautiously. "I think it would be better if the two of you had time alone. He probably has a lot to say and he'd feel more comfortable without me there."

Janet picked up her jacket and the car keys. "All right. I'll see you later?"

"Count on it."

He listened to her heels tapping on the wooden floor until the sound became too faint to hear. Walking to the window, he watched her get into the car and drive away. He'd known her only a matter of days, but she was fast becoming a part of his life. Did she feel anything for him? He knew how she responded to him in bed, but was that lust or love she was experiencing? He wished he knew.

Even more, he wished he knew why it was so important to him.

Eight

It was almost dark when Janet returned to the inn, and the overcast day had fulfilled its promise. It was pouring. Peter had missed all his classes, as their talk had gone on long after the luncheon dishes had been cleared away. She had *her* Peter back, and she swore that she would never let anything come between them again. She'd learned from her mistake, and had made him the promise that she would never hold back from him again, no matter how unpleasant the subject might be. He'd told her he loved her and wanted to be part of her life.

He'd also told her about his meeting with Ken.

As she was about to make her way up the stairs she sighed, sagging against the banister. The main room was deserted and the heavy patter of the rain tapped a solemn song on the old windows, but still she procrastinated, unsure of what she should say to Ken. She was exhausted. The emotional ups and down of the day left her as wrung out as yesterday's wash. She wasn't looking forward to a confrontation with him, but felt one was necessary to get her point across.

And what was her point? Part of her shouted, "Don't interfere in my life!" While another, more gentle, rational side only wanted to thank him for whatever it was he'd said to her stepson to make him change his mind. She supposed the point was very basic: Ken had taken it on himself to make a decision that would affect her life. Maybe that was why it bothered her so. He'd done to her exactly what she'd done to Peter. He hadn't lied about seeing Peter this morning; he just hadn't told her. It would be hypocritical of her to reprimand Ken for helping her. And it *had* all turned out for the best.

But what if it hadn't? What if he'd completely alienated Peter from her? What if she'd lost him forever?

These realizations brought home Peter's feelings of betrayal with striking clarity. While what Ken had done was minor in comparison, he still had done her thinking for her, manipulated her, taken away her free will to say no.

Peter had been right to be furious. It hurt like hell.

Janet pushed herself away from the railing and continued up the stairs. She wanted only to soak in a hot tub, eat something, because she'd never really touched a bit of her lunch, and climb into that feather-soft bed to cuddle within a pair of warm, solid, hair-roughened arms. She breathed deeply at the thought, the wish, and sighed before opening the door to the room.

The sight that greeted her once more threw her emotions out of kilter. Ken stood by the window, dressed only in light blue, faded jeans that rode low on his hips. He was half-hidden in the shadows, with only the dim rays of lamplight casting an inviting streak across the bed.

"Hi," he said.

Janet stepped into the room and closed the door behind her. "Hi."

"How did it go?"

"Fine," she answered. "Great, really! He poured out his heart to me. We settled a lot. Whatever changed his mind has my eternal gratitude." She waited for him to pick up on her opening and confess.

"Don't try to analyze it," he said quietly.

"I don't really have to, do I, Ken?" She walked closer to him; she wanted to see his eyes when she asked. "Why didn't you tell me you went to see him this morning?"

Ken looked at her for a moment, then turned his face away before walking toward the bed. He put down a glass she hadn't noticed he'd been holding.

"So he told you."

"Did you think he wouldn't?"

"I didn't know. I didn't even know if what I had to say sank in at all. He was very noncommittal. For all I knew, it might have made things worse."

"That's the point, isn't it, Ken? What if it *had* made things worse? It wasn't your place to get involved in this. You can't play with people's lives."

Ken looked up at her and their gazes held.

"I know what you're going to say," she began. "I've already berated myself for what I did to Peter. But don't you see that you did the same thing to me?"

"Yes," Ken answered. "I do. And I'm sorry. But at the time, I was so furious. I just couldn't stand by and watch you crumble. I thought I had something to say to the kid that might work. And it did."

"Yes, it worked. But you should have told me. You should have given me the option to say yes or no." Janet shook her head and turned her back to him, staring out the window into the blackness of the night. "All my life, I've had people telling me what to do. First at the orphanage, then the foster homes. J.D. was practically my *keeper*, for heaven's sake!" She swung back around to face him. "I'm not complaining. It's how I chose to live with him. It was what I needed then." She walked up to him and stopped inches away. "But it's not what I need now."

Ken reached up and brushed a few damp tendrils of hair away from her face. His touch was soft, gentle, almost a caress.

"I know. And I'm sorry. I should have told you. Maybe I even would have if you hadn't jumped all over me when I came into the room. I don't know. I do know what you're saying, though, and I promise you, I'll never do anything behind your back again."

Janet covered his hand with hers, savoring his warmth.

"It's funny. That's basically the same thing I said to Peter this afternoon. An awful lot of promises were made today. I hope we can keep them."

"We can if we try. If we want to."

He kissed her forehead. "I'm glad it worked out all right."

"So am I."

He took both her hands in his and rubbed them. "You're freezing! And you look like a wet rag."

"Thanks for the compliment. I'd argue, except that's exactly how I feel."

He helped her out of her jacket and pulled her along after him, leading her into the bathroom.

"What...?"

Inside, the old porcelain claw-foot tub was filled with steaming water.

"Ken, are you psychic?"

He laughed. "I saw you pull up. When you got out of the car, you looked as if this was exactly what you needed. Go ahead, try it out. I have a surprise for you."

"What kind of surprise?"

"Patience," he said, and left her alone to contemplate his cryptic remark.

Janet stared, hands on hips, at the bathroom door as he closed it on his way out. He was the most confusing, complex man she'd ever met. She'd been so reluctant to have that conversation with him, thinking he would be defensive. Instead, surprisingly, he'd agreed with her, as if they shared the very same thoughts and opinions. She sensed that strength was always there, close to the surface, along with a kindness that wasn't threatened by it, only enhanced. She shook her head, deciding her state of mind this evening wasn't conducive to figuring him out. She should relax and enjoy him.

She dipped her hand into the water, testing the temperature. It was just right. But of course. Everything he did seemed to be just right for her. No. Perfect. Just perfect.

Janet threw off her clothes and got into the tub, wrapping her worn-out body in the cocoon of water, allowing it to cast a spell over her as its warmth penetrated and melted away her fatigue. Her eyelashes fluttered closed and she could almost feel the tensions of the day ooze from her pores.

The water had barely cooled, when her nose began to twitch in reaction to the bubbles. She opened her eyes to find a pair of deep dark ones boring into her own.

"Take a sip," Ken ordered, holding a very thin, fragile crystal flute glass filled with champagne to her mouth.

Janet complied, her eyes never leaving Ken's as he tipped the glass slightly and the chilled, biting liquid slid down her throat.

"I thought I'd take a chance and order it, hoping we'd have something to celebrate tonight."

"What a treat!" she said. "I've never been served champagne this way before."

"I should hope not," he said in all sincerity.

Janet supposed she should feel embarrassed with him sitting there on the edge of the tub, but she didn't. It felt like the most natural thing in the world.

"What's that?" She pointed to a bite-sized morsel he held between his thumb and forefinger.

"Taste it and find out."

She warned him with her eyes as she opened her mouth to accept his offering, and nipped his fingers as her teeth grazed the soft pad on his thumb. The smoldering look in his eyes told her he didn't mind. At all.

"Shrimp?"

"Shrimp."

"Mmm, good." She opened her mouth for another piece.

"I thought you had lunch," he said as he fed her.

She shook her head as she chewed. "I was too excited to eat. I'm starving."

Ken held the dish out in front of her and she continued to consume its contents.

"I'm glad everything worked out between you and Peter."

She smiled up at him. "So am I. I feel as if the weight of the world has been lifted off my shoulders." She pointed to the champagne glass he held. "May I have another sip?"

He tilted the glass to her lips and as she drank, his eyes roamed her face.

"He liked you, you know," she said, and Ken grinned.

"Oh, yeah? What did he say?"

"He said you seemed like an 'okay guy.' That's pretty heavy stuff for Peter!"

Ken laughed. "Did you invite him home?"

"Yes. The weekend before Thanksgiving. He's spending the holiday with Katherine. Then we'll have him for Christmas break. Is that okay with you?"

"Fine. We'll have to plan something special to do."

Janet smacked her lips at the tartness of the champagne as she finished off the glass.

"Did you have enough, milady?" Ken teased.

"Yes, thank you, sir."

Ken took hold of her hand and helped her to a standing position in the tub while he unfolded a large terry bath towel. He wrapped it around her shoulders and lifted her out of the water. He held her to him for a long moment before allowing her feet to touch the tile floor. She didn't move away. She didn't want to.

Janet adjusted the towel as he silently led her out of the bathroom over to the bed. He sat on the edge and pulled her to stand between his legs. He began to move the towel over her, gently blotting the drops of water, seemingly one at a time.

"What are you doing?" she asked.

"Drying you."

"I'm perfectly capable of drying myself."

"I'm sure you are. But this is Lesson One in your sorely lacking education. Have you ever had a man do this for you?"

Janet swallowed, her once-chilled skin beginning to take on a warm glow. "I can't say that I have."

"Then allow me to be the first," he said, as his tongue swirled around one dusty pink, pouting nipple, "and the last."

His lips closed around her. He suckled one breast, then the other, his hot, wet mouth searing her flesh as he moved back and forth. Her knees buckled and he caught her in his arms, first cradling her body against his, then slowly lowering her to the cool cotton sheets.

Ken leaned over her, his dark eyes roaming her face, trapping her as effectively as his arms around her body. Wordlessly he brought his lips to hers. She tasted of champagne, shrimp and Janet, the combination as intoxicating as any mixture he'd ever experienced.

He released her mouth and grinned at her as he traced his finger along her brow.

"This isn't going as planned," he said.

Janet swallowed. She thought it was going just fine.

"Oh?" She cleared her throat. "What was the plan?"

"The *plan* was to give you a long, relaxing massage, after which you'd lose all those doubts of yours and fall willingly into my arms."

She chuckled. "Sounds wonderful. Should I fight you off now and we'll begin again?"

"No. I don't think so."

He sat up and walked to the dresser. Janet sat up and watched the play of muscles on his back. Her resolve not to make love with him was fast evaporating, and she was having a hard time remembering why it was so important to resist him in the first place.

Ken returned to the bed and directed her to lay on her stomach. The bath towel tangled around her torso as she complied. Something cold slid down the middle of her back and she called out in surprise.

"Relax," he said. "It's only body lotion."

He ran his hands through the liquid and began to spread it impersonally in broad strokes over her shoulder blades and lower back. Janet moaned as her muscles protested, then she allowed her body to gc limp in response to the strong, intense massage. The aroma of the lotion reached her and she breathed in the smell of lanolin with a hint of coconut. Ken's hands moved to her arms, all the way to her fingers, then with long sweeping motions back down to her lower back.

"I feel like a bowl of melting butter," she murmured, eyes closed in ecstasy.

Ken leaned forward, his breath feathering her ear. "Good. That's the way I want you—creamy soft and ready to—"

"Careful!" she warned, a smile in her voice.

He laughed and moved back toward the end of the bed.

He picked up her ankle and began to massage first one foot, then the other, gliding his hands up to her calves, then her thighs, kneading the aches away.

Then his touch began to change. Gone were the strong, sure movements. He began a slower, gentler caress. His fingers grew bold and touched her intimately. Her body squirmed as a fire began to smolder in the pit of her belly.

Ken lifted his hands from her and sat back. It took Janet a moment to realize he'd stopped. She opened her eyes and twisted around to look at him. His eyes were bright, fathomless, and his face a rigid mask of self-control.

"You said something about promises tonight." His voice was low and raspy. "I've made one to you, and I'll keep it. If you want me to."

Janet turned completely onto her back, the towel pulling away, leaving her naked to his view. Without hesitation, she held out her arms to him. He fell forward, his arms outstretched on either side of her, caging her between them. He wanted to tell her how much this meant to him, but the raging fire inside caused the words to stick in his throat, so he continued only to stare.

She reached up and stroked his face. "Ken, I want you. But I'm not using any protection—"

"Let me take care of it." When she nodded, he asked, "Are you sure this is what you want? Because God help me, once I touch you again, I won't be able to stop."

Janet's gaze roamed his face, the taut muscles of his arms, the springy hair on his chest, then returned magnetically to his eyes. A tenderness tugged at her heart at the sight of this man gazing down at her with desire and passion battling for control of his body. She wanted to absorb him, touch that very part of him that made him what he was. The feeling was so powerful, so intense, it almost consumed her. She cupped his face with two shaking hands.

"Come to me," she whispered. "I want to feel you inside me, a part of me. Please."

Moving away, he quickly divested himself of his jeans and protected himself before returning to the bed and her open arms. His body was hot as he lowered himself onto her. He kissed her, a sweet kiss, more of a promise than a deed. He raised his face slightly to look into her eyes. And then, eyes locked to hers, he entered her welcoming warmth. She was so ready for him he groaned as shudders racked his body.

Janet gasped at the initial invasion, then lifted her hips to accept him fully, desperate for more of him, all of him. All her bridled longing burst forth in this one action. A storm brewed between them, and they rode it out together, rising and falling in waves until their bodies responded to the tumult.

Ken buried his face in the hollow of her neck, murmuring love words of praise as he brought them both to a rare, simultaneous climax.

They didn't move. There was no need. His weight was as welcome as the deep, sealing kiss he gave her. Janet had never been more relaxed in her life, and as she felt reality slip away under the cover of sleep, she thought she heard him whisper, "I love you."

But then again, maybe she dreamed it.

Nine

Ken had just about had it. After blowing his top with Edmund for the way he'd interfered with his call to Janet, he'd politely listened to the lecture about his responsibility to the company and the family. But what about his responsibility to himself?

"No more, Edmund." Ken gestured with his hand as he headed for the door. "I'm getting out of here before this gets out of hand and we both say things we'll be sorry for later."

"This wasn't part of the agreement."

Ken's hand froze on the doorknob as Edmund's words stopped him cold.

Edmund stood behind the desk in the study. Ken looked at his brother's face and knew that the events of the evening had wreaked havoc with Edmund's blood pressure. Edmund couldn't understand his defense of his new wife. He realized Edmund's dislike of Janet wasn't personal. It was all business to him, and when it came to Radnor Corporation, he had tunnel vision. Ken loved his brother, and experienced a momentary surge of guilt because what he was about to say would only upset him more. But say it he must, for the words were begging to be spoken, even if he hadn't completely acknowledged them himself. Ken returned to his seat and in a low, controlled voice replied to his brother's comment.

"I know it wasn't, Edmund. But we can't always plan when and with whom we fall in love."

Edmund's eyes widened in shocked surprise. "You're in love with her?"

"I'm beginning to think so."

"I can't believe this of you, Kenneth! Brian, yes, but you?"

"What is it, Ed? Why are you so against this marriage working? Why can't you picture me with a wife, a family, like you and Eleanor? I'm not a machine. I need a life, too, just like everyone else."

"You never have before. I suppose I'm used to you always being here for me, for the company."

"I'm still here for you and the company. Nothing will change. The only thing different is that now I have someone to love, to share my life with. Is that too difficult for you to accept?"

"Of course not! I certainly don't begrudge you your happiness. It's just that—" Edmund stopped, seemingly uncertain about how to continue.

"Spit it out, Edmund. You've never been shy with me before. Don't start now."

"All right, I will. I won't interfere with your love life if you want to pursue this marriage, but I just can't tolerate the thought of Janet sitting on our board of directors with voting rights."

Ken sighed audibly and shook his head. "Is that all that's bothering you?"

"For the moment."

"If I get Janet to sign over the stock to me, will that make you happy?"

"Completely. But do you think you can convince her to do it?"

"I don't see why not. Unlike you, I believe she's not interested in this just for the money. I'm vain enough to think I have more than a little to do with it."

Ken rose and headed for the door, anxious to end the conversation. It was dinner time and he hadn't seen Janet all day. He wanted to go up to their rooms and kiss her hello, have dinner with her, spend a quiet evening at home. Just like an everyday, ordinary married couple.

When they arrived back from upstate this morning, he'd gone straight to the office. It amazed him how much time he'd spent today thinking about her, about them. He found himself leaving the office at the end of the day, instead of staying until eight or nine o'clock, as was his usual habit. In less than a week, she'd changed his life. The thought didn't disturb him, as perhaps it should have. Instead he felt as if he were at the brink of something wonderful, and he had a definite urge to jump in first and think later.

Edmund's parting comment stopped him.

"I'd like this settled as soon as possible. Especially in light of what Douglas Carmichael now knows. I want the stock in our hands, and yesterday wouldn't be soon enough as far as I'm concerned."

Ken nodded. Carmichael and the stock. Would they never go away and leave him alone? The two were intertwined in an intricate web that now had another victim: Janet.

"Hello everyone!" Ken announced as he entered the dining room.

The children immediately began to chatter, each vying for his sole attention. He acknowledged them as his eyes sought and found Janet.

"I missed you," he whispered in her ear as he took his seat next to her.

Her face glowing, Janet looked across the table and returned Brian's grin and conspiratorial wink. They'd met in the garden for the first time that afternoon and had hit it off right away. Everything she'd heard about the youngest Radnor was true—he was playfully outrageous, and a lot of fun. It was good to have him there for support.

She glanced at Ken as he played with the children, working with their competitiveness and fueling their animated talk. He was the center of attention, and as she watched him, a silly smile was plastered on her face. She knew it was there, but couldn't for the life of her make it go away. An urge born of desire beckoned her to touch him in some way—perhaps only his hand. But she held back, savoring the anticipation. Soon, when dinner was over, she would have her wish.

The day had been endless without him, and she'd found herself replaying the events at the inn over and over in her mind. It was impossible, even now, to forget his touch, his taste. The food seemed mediocre in comparison. She had a hunger of a different kind tonight.

At one point during dinner their gazes locked, and Ken's fork froze midway at the message she was sending. She'd never known the power of her sexuality, and the realization was exhilarating as well as a little frightening.

The sound of her name brought her out of her self-imposed daze.

"Janet? What do you think? Are you interested?" Brian asked.

She focused on him across the table. "I—I'm sorry, Brian. I didn't hear the question."

Brian tilted his head and grinned. "I was suggesting to everyone that since they're putting me in charge of the national business, we need a new administrator for the office. You've taken some business administration courses, haven't you?"

"Yes, I have, but—"

"And was office management part of that?"

"Yes, but—"

"Then I hereby nominate Mrs. Janet Radnor for the position of office administrator for Radnor Corporation."

"Now wait one minute, Brian! We never discussed—"

"What's to discuss, Edmund? Janet would be perfect for the job. She's got the background. She's a member of the family. It's an ideal way for her to keep busy and it would sure save me the hassle of having to interview to hire someone new."

Janet stared at Brian in disbelief. This was a total surprise to her. She turned to study Ken's face for his reaction, but his pensive expression told her nothing. The thought of working every day by his side shot a modicum of excitement through her. The company obviously meant a great deal to him. Perhaps if she learned something about his business, she would learn something about the man in the process. Her own job at the university would pose no problem, as she'd already taken a leave of absence for this school term. What harm would it do to try out Brian's suggestion, if only for a short while? She looked back to Ken again, trying to discern his mood.

"I think it's a great idea," Ken said, wondering how he would ever get any work done with her in the office all day. "How do you feel about it, Janet?"

"I don't know. I'd like to think about it."

"Why not come into the office tomorrow," Brian said, "and we can go over the job description. You'd be able to get an idea of what it's all about."

"Now let's talk about this some more here," Edmund interrupted. "There are many, many things we need to discuss before we make a decision about—"

"Stow it, Edmund," Ken ordered. Childish as it seemed, Edmund's protest only seemed to solidify Ken's approval. "It's settled. If Janet agrees, she can start tomorrow. I'll bring her down to the office myself. Okay?" he asked her.

"Okay," she answered, to everyone's delight.

Everyone, that is, except Edmund. The scowl he directed at her could only be termed ominous. Apprehension shot down her spine at the force of it, effectively breaking her bubble. What could she be thinking? She had to remember who she was and why she was here. There was still the stock they all wanted from her. And *all* included Ken. It would be wise to keep that thought uppermost in her mind. Because as much as Ken and Brian and the others made her feel welcome, she was essentially still a stranger. Edmund knew that, accepted that. Why couldn't she?

For when push came to shove, and she knew someday it must, whose side would Ken take? Hers? Or Edmund's?

The sobering thought brought her up short, making her realize she was truly alone in this...this...situation. Should she go to the office tomorrow and learn all she could? Knowledge was power, and she had a feeling she might need all the power she could get.

Janet paced the room. She'd left Ken downstairs, talking to Brian, and knew he would be up momentarily. They needed to have a talk of their own. The more she rehashed Edmund's reaction to her working at Radnor Corporation, the more convinced she was that perhaps they were rushing into this. Edmund had made it perfectly clear he didn't want her involved. No matter how many times Ken made love with her, it didn't change the fact that he, too, wanted the stock. The question was, did he want *it* more than her?

Ken entered the room without knocking, and found Janet sitting on the love seat, deep in thought. "Hi," he said.

Janet looked up at him. The face above her was content, affectionate. His eyes roamed her features, as if searching for something he'd yet to find. He almost looked as if he...no, it couldn't be. She was only imagining what she so desperately wanted to see, reading emotions into his eyes that really weren't there. She had to stop this obsession with him and get down to business. She stood, if not to put her on equal terms, then at least to lessen the difference.

"Hi." She returned his greeting curtly, without looking at him.

Ken was puzzled. She was definitely miffed at something. He'd practically run up the stairs, anxious beyond belief to hold her, kiss her, make love with her. It was what he'd thought about, waited for, all day. She'd seemed so receptive earlier. What could have changed since dinner?

"Something wrong?" he asked.

"You tell me."

"Are we back to playing word games, Janet? I thought we'd progressed beyond that."

"No games, Ken, word or otherwise. You tell me. What's behind this offer for me to work at Radnor Corporation?"

"There's nothing behind it. Brian told you everything. We need a new administrator." He moved closer toward her. "And what does that have to do with your attitude toward me? What the hell happened since dinner? For God's sake, look at me when I talk to you."

Janet spun toward him, her eyes angry, determined. "My attitude is the same toward you as toward the rest of your family. Don't you understand? I'm the outsider. I'm the one everyone looks at and sees dollar signs! My attitude is a direct result of yours, nothing more or less. Edmund hates me—" She held up her hand when he started to interrupt. "Don't tell me it's not so. I can feel it. And let's face it, bottom line, the only thing any of you want from me is the stock!"

She turned away from him again, refusing to stare into those dark, brooding eyes that promised so much. She had to force herself to look away before she gave in. The touch of his hand on her shoulder was feather light as he turned her toward him. He was so close she could feel the heat of his body radiating to her. She kept her head down, but was unable to move from his heat.

"The stock isn't the only thing I want from you, Janet, and you know it." He raised her chin with his hand. "Look at me. Look into my eyes. Tell me you believe that all I want you for is a block of stock. Tell me what you see, Janet."

She gazed deeply into his eyes, and what she saw frightened her all the more for its power. No, he couldn't feel this way about her, not so soon. Her mind cried out its warnings, but her heart beat double time at the thoughts and feelings his eyes evoked.

"Tell me..." he urged, bringing her closer until their bodies touched.

Her insides trembled at the contact. Was it possible to physically want someone this much? To crave a man so? To be addicted to him as one is to a drug? Her insides were melting with longing and desire. And he was only looking at her. What would happen when he kissed her...?

"You know what I feel," he whispered, his lips barely an inch from hers. "You feel it, too. Don't fight it, Janet. Don't throw it away...please..."

Ken's lips brushed against hers as he entreated. She opened her mouth to him, and he took full advantage of the opportunity and plundered the sweet secrets within. Janet clung to him, digging her nails into his jacket, kneading the muscles of his shoulders beneath, the feeling of his strength as overpowering and intoxicating as his taste.

He released her mouth and continued to press kisses down her neck, around her ear. The chills came in waves, over and over, until she could hardly stand. She wanted him so much she ached inside. She had to stop now, before it was too late, before they ceased to think at all.

Janet pushed against him. He let her go, but didn't move away. Ken realized she needed talk now more than lovemaking, even though it wasn't what either wanted. He walked to the portable bar and poured himself a brandy.

"Okay. Let's talk."

Janet sat in the chair and watched as he took a gulp of the brandy and ran his fingers through his hair. It was sticking up in the back and she fought the urge to smooth it down. She looked away. Looking at him did no good; it only confused her.

"We have a contract," she began. "A business arrangement that just happens, in our case, to include marriage. But it's not a real marriage. We didn't even know each other before the day of the wedding—''

"This is old news, Janet. We both understood the rules before we met. But we *have* met. We've made love. We're falling in love." He shook his head. "Don't deny it. It's there and you know it as well as I do. I'd like to know why you won't nurture that love. Why are you constantly sabotaging what we feel?"

Janet sighed, both warmed and chilled by his words. "You didn't let me finish. I was trying to explain why I feel the way I do. I'm not consciously sabotaging a relationship between us. You have to understand that I can't be sure if what you say you feel is genuine or if it's prompted by your desire to own all the stock."

"Back to the stock again, is it?"

"We've never been very far away from it, Ken. That's the point I've been trying to make. It's always there, standing between us. And I'm sorry, but I can't wish it away or pretend it doesn't exist."

"If it wasn't for the stock, then, where would be be?"

"Free. Free to do what comes naturally," she answered wistfully.

Ken walked toward her and plunked his brandy glass down on the coffee table. "Then sign the stock over to me."

"What?"

"You heard me. Sign the stock over to me and I'll sign an agreement to personally pay you when the company has the cash flow."

Janet stared at him incredulously. Did he really think her that stupid that she would give up her one and only bargaining chip in this strange game?

"I couldn't possibly do that, Ken, and you know it."

"Why not? It would solve all our problems."

"It would solve all *your* problems, you mean!"

"Afraid I'll cheat you?"

Janet faced him. "If I were only concerned with myself, Kenneth Radnor, I wouldn't even be having this ridiculous conversation with you to begin with. You fail to realize, or are too thick to understand that I don't need your money. I can take care of myself. But I made a promise to J.D. and have a responsibility to Peter. It's his money, too. And I'm not about to sign anything over to you or anyone else until he's taken care of."

She turned away from him and headed toward the bedroom. His voice stopped her in the doorway.

"Then what you're saying is that you don't trust me."

"I don't trust any of you."

"But me in particular. Correct?"

Janet shrugged, choosing to ignore the cold, calculating look in his eyes as she answered. "Yes."

Ken headed for the exit, resigned to spending the night in Brian's rooms. He took hold of the doorknob and turned it slowly, the clicking sound echoing in the suddenly silent room. Janet stood stock still in the bedroom doorway, following his every movement in that strong yet vulnerable way of hers. Well, at least now he knew the score.

"Then we'll have to do something about that, won't we, Janet?" Not giving her a chance to answer his cryptic remark, he opened the door and was gone.

She'd won. She'd made her point and held her own with him. She'd been strong and clear with him; levelheaded and succinct. She was her own person, and didn't need him or anyone else.

Janet walked into the room and sat down on the bed. She ran her hand over the soft satin comforter and fell back, staring at the ceiling.

So why wasn't she elated? Why did she feel miserable, lonely and abandoned? And why was sleeping in this great, big bed alone with "her own person," not half as appealing as sharing it with him?

The knock on the door woke her. She glanced at the clock on the nightstand and saw that it was only seven-fifteen in the morning—too early for the maid to make the bed. The knocking persisted. She quickly donned the mauve satin robe that lay crumpled at the foot of the bed. She opened the door to find Ken leaning against the wall, his suit jacket slung over his shoulder, tie hanging unknotted around his neck and shirt halfway buttoned. Her gaze was drawn to the thick mat of chest hair visible through the shirt opening, and she looked away. Her nerve endings were barely awake and totally unprepared to cope with any physical feelings he provoked.

"Why aren't you dressed?"

"Dressed?"

"Yes, Janet, you know, clothes on the body—dressed."

He brushed past her and walked into the middle of the room.

"Are we supposed to be going somewhere?" she asked.

"The office. Today's your first day on the job. Or have you forgotten?"

"No, I haven't forgotten. I just thought, well, after last night, you and I—"

"What happens between you and me has nothing to do with the business. I thought I made that clear."

"That's what you *said*, but—"

"And I mean what I say," he told her pointedly. "Someday you'll believe that."

She was at a loss for words. He was so in command this morning, so businesslike. She didn't know what to make of it. It was so good to drink in the sight of him that she allowed herself the luxury for a moment more. His chest moved slightly as he breathed and the tufts of hair beckoned for her to touch. She closed her eyes tightly for a split second to clear her head. When she opened them, her eyes met his, a lingering look that asked and answered countless questions in a single heartbeat.

"Get dressed," he ordered softly, his voice tinged with regret, as if that were the last thing he wanted her to do.

She moved past him, her robe grazing his legs as she went by. Ken closed his eyes. There'd been a definite look of longing in her eyes. He'd felt the force of it jolt his body. Why was she fighting him? Why couldn't she sign over that damn stock and free them both, free them to love each other the way it was meant to be? He had to convince her, prove to her it was the right thing to do. He had to make her trust him, want him, love him, as much as he did her. He hated this powerless feeling.

He went downstairs and finished dressing in front of the hallway mirror, returning to the dining room for a cup of coffee. Janet walked in soon after, and he marveled at the transformation from sleepy waif to prim businesswoman. She was dressed in a dove-gray suit with a bright pink blouse. The suit was tailored to fit perfectly and was in no way seductive, but his imagination was fertile and he knew what lay under those serious clothes. He watched as she poured herself a cup of coffee from the buffet and placed a sweet roll in the small plate. She sat across from him, eyes down as she ate her breakfast, calm, cool and collected for all the world to see.

But he knew better. The pulse on the side of her neck throbbed with a life of its own. He remembered how he'd kissed that small pulse as he made his way to nuzzle her ear. He remembered how it tasted, its texture and how it told him of the racing of her blood as it kept time with his own.

Janet looked up and caught him smiling—a silly grin, really—and wondered what he saw. She reached up and touched her neck, feeling flustered by the knowing look in his eye. He was making her nervous, and she didn't know why. The grin became a smirk, and she could feel the blush begin to creep up to her cheeks.

"Are you ready?" he asked.

She dared not be coy and ask "For what?" and nodded her agreement.

They arrived soon after at the office complex. The receptionist's effusive greeting was a prelude of more to come, and Janet tried to be as gracious as possible. As she walked down the corridor with Ken, men and women emerged from their offices to slap his back and shake her hand and wish both of them happiness in their new life. Ken moved her along quickly without being rude, and ushered her into his office at the end of the long hallway.

He walked over to the desk and began to peruse his mail and messages, as Janet observed the room. It was big—big enough to hold a conference. But it bore the mark of a professional decorator who'd never met the man for whom it was intended. The glass-and-chrome desk and chrome-and-leather chairs were masculine in a prissy sort of way, she supposed, but they weren't Ken. His size dwarfed the short, fat ferns oddly arranged around the room, and he— or they—seemed out of place. She stopped herself from asking his permission to redecorate when she realized she probably would be long gone before the furniture was even delivered.

Brian walked into the office unannounced. "Morning," he said. "I've come to fetch Janet." He smiled at her. "Ready to go to work?"

"Yes, sir," she answered, with a backward glance to Ken.

Ken dropped the envelopes he was holding and stared at her. He hesitated before taking a step toward her. For a minute, it looked as if he was going to kiss her.

Janet swayed forward, wanting him to.

Instead, he stepped back, as if he thought better of it.

"Good luck," he said, as Brian ushered her out of the room. "I'll be in my office if you need anything from me."

She nodded and followed Brian out the door. What she needed from him couldn't be found in the office.

Janet had never been this busy in her life. The day raced by at an alarming pace. She and Brian were so involved in the office manual that she was unable to break for lunch. It was dark when they'd finished, after six, and Brian had dashed off to who knows where, leaving her alone in his office. She shut the huge book and clicked off the desk lamp, rolling her neck left and right as she stood, working out the kinks. She was exhausted but exhilarated at the same time. Working in an office was so different from working with students. There was an air of urgency in everything that happened here. People had run in and out of Brian's office all day long with such diverse problems it made her head spin. She wasn't sure if she could handle this on a daily basis all by herself, but part of her wanted to try.

After refreshing herself in Brian's private bathroom, Janet made her way through the maze of offices in search of Ken. She found him, hunched over, elbows on desk, completely engrossed in the material contained in a manila folder. He didn't hear her approach and she took the time to observe him unnoticed. The sight of him made her blood pump faster. She wondered if she would ever become immune to him.

In between all the work that day, she'd made time to think about what Ken had said to her the night before. Perhaps he was right; perhaps she *was* sabotaging their relationship. She wanted to explore the possibilities with him, without the intrusion of the office and the family.

Sensing someone at the door, Ken looked up and stared intently at the vision before him. Knowing she was only down the hall all day had brought her to mind with increasing frequency. Instead of clouding his thoughts, however, the knowledge had soothed him. Odd as it seemed, it was comforting to know she was a mere step or two away. It had egged him on to get going with his work, to complete it quickly and efficiently so that more time could be spent with her.

Janet smiled as his face relaxed. It warmed her to know she affected him as much as he did her. She knew this decision to give their growing love a chance was a risky one. Her emotions were very fragile. But the alternative—being without him—was too awful to contemplate.

"Can I buy you dinner, sailor?" she teased.

Ken leaned back in his leather swivel chair, the springs cushioning his weight as he rocked slowly back and forth. Janet leaned against the doorway as she deliberately flirted with him. He was enamored, and too relieved to question her light mood. He gave in to it as the sight and sound of her titillated his senses.

"Come on over here and we'll discuss it."

Janet heard the smoke in his voice and moved slowly. Her own need for him propelled her toward him as surely as his husky, sensuous voice drew her. When she stood in front of him, he took her hand and guided her onto his lap.

"It's been heaven and hell knowing you were so near all day," he said, his eyes roaming her face.

She stared deeply into the bright darkness and felt a thrill at all she saw. "I know."

"Do you? I wonder."

Janet touched his face, gently outlining his brow with the tips of her fingers. He was warm to the touch, and so inviting. She fought the urge to plunge both hands into his hair. "Don't," she whispered.

"Don't what?"

"Wonder."

She dipped her head and pressed her lips to his. She held onto his shoulder for support as the initial contact shot a spasm of pure pleasure throughout her body. The taste and smell of him combined to make her head spin, senses reel, as an indefensible onslaught of emotion battered her.

Ken wrapped his arms around her and cradled her head. Their tongues touched and mated, spinning them both out of control. She squirmed on his lap in an effort to get closer, and the jolt to his system was so fierce, so potent, he almost dropped her.

"Oh, sweetheart," he said, "I want you so much."

He kneaded her back with strong hands, the undulating motion bringing her closer as his lips scorched her neck.

She was pliable to his touch, and he felt her body go slack with desire. Something primal urged him to lift her onto the desk and take her now, while she was so soft and warm and willing—

The background sound of the vacuum triggered the rational side of his brain, and he slowed down, as cold realization reminded him of where they were. Janet was once again on her feet before her own mind registered the fact that Ken had stopped kissing her. She was dazed, the dim cloud of desire obscuring her vision.

"The cleaning people," he explained.

"Oh..." she murmured. The blood was still pumping rapidly through her veins. What was wrong with her? Every time the man looked at her, touched her, kissed her, she crumbled. It wasn't to be believed the way he only had to crook a finger to have her panting like a dog in heat.

"Let's go home," he suggested.

If they went home, they would be in bed five minutes after they hit the door. She wanted to spend some time with him. Talking time.

Janet shook her head. "Not home. Not yet. Let me buy dinner."

"On one condition."

"What's that?"

"I get to pick dessert."

Ten

The restaurant was small, dark and intimate. Soft music drifted in from the lounge. The tables were round and compact, and their knees touched underneath as their hands caressed above. Janet made a mental note to thank Brian for his suggestion. She was happy and heady with the wine as well as the company.

"How was your day?" Ken asked. "I apologize for not being able to stop in to see you, but first days back in the office after a trip are always hectic, to say the least."

"I was fine. Brian took excellent care of me. I must admit, though, that I never knew how *involved* your business was! We spent hours just going over the manual...all those specifications! I'll never remember any of them."

"You won't have to. All you need is a working knowledge of what's needed when inquiries come in on bids. The office personnel know their jobs very well and handle all the technical stuff. We need you to maintain it all, keep order and make sure everyone is happy.''

"Brian did listen to an awful lot of personal problems today. I was surprised that people would confide that way with an employer.'' She took a sip of wine as they accepted menus from the waiter.

"It's a family business, Janet. Some of these people have been with us for over thirty years. We try to make them feel as much a part of it as possible.''

For a fleeting moment, Janet envied the security he took for granted. "You're very lucky to have grown up with all this.''

"I know that,'' he said. "It's quite a support system.''

She leaned forward, elbows on the table. "Tell me about it.''

Ken studied her face. He would love to open up to her, to tell her about his life, his hopes, his dreams. He wondered if she really wanted to hear them.

"We grew up with very specific rules. My parents taught us to depend on one another. What we learned was that family ties were the only ones that couldn't be broken.''

Janet watched his eyes cloud over. "You seem to believe that.''

"I do,'' he said. "It's been proven to me time and again. Others come and go. Your family is the only constant in life. In mine, anyway.''

"What about your first wife?''

Ken laughed out loud. "Marcia? No. 'Constant' isn't a word I'd associate with her. Unless it was constant complaining. There was never enough of anything for Marcia.''

"You sound bitter.''

"Do I? I don't mean to. She taught me a very important lesson early enough in life to have a good effect.

Marrying her was my one impulsive act. It backfired. I paid for it—financially and emotionally. I'm a better person for it." He became serious. "But it's been more than a dozen years, Janet. I rarely, if ever, think about that time in my life."

"There's been no one else, then?" she asked, surprised at how interested she was in his answer.

"You mean romantically?"

"Yes. You know, girlfriends."

Ken shook his head. "I have many woman friends. Some may have been more intimate friends than others, but to answer your question, no, there haven't been any serious relationships." Until you, he added to himself.

"Oh."

He grinned. "'Oh'? Just 'oh'? No comment?"

Janet gestured with her hands. "I guess I find it odd that a man like you hasn't had a woman in his life all these years."

"I didn't say I haven't had any women in my life. I said none of the relationships have been serious. There's a difference, Janet."

She lowered her gaze from his unsettling one. "I see. Your relationship with your family is emotionally satisfying enough. You don't need any other. Is that right?"

Her comment shook him. He'd never thought about it that way, but perhaps she had a point. Did his family meet all his needs, save the obvious sexual one? He wasn't sure if he liked that image of himself.

"I never said that. No one is that self-sufficient. Not even me. Having a close family is one thing. Sharing your life with someone is something else entirely," he said, caressing the side of her face. *Share mine with me,* he said to himself.

She read more in his eyes than in his words. She wanted to believe what those eyes were saying, but she was afraid to be wrong, to be hurt. To be left out in the cold again, after all these years, would be devastating to her emotionally.

Trust was such a hard thing to come by, much harder in some ways than love.

Ken sat back in his chair leaving a short distance between them. "So, do you think you'd like to join us?"

Janet sighed, shaking away the morose thoughts. "I loved the work. It was so different for me, and definitely a challenge, but I really don't know, Ken. It's only been one day, and to tell the truth, I'm a little overwhelmed by it all. I made a commitment to Dr. Franklin at the university that I'd return, at least for next semester, and I couldn't disappoint him...." She hesitated to continue.

"And?" he prodded.

"And neither of us knows how long I'll be here."

Ken studied her. Her doubts about him were strong; he couldn't deny that. He also couldn't deny his equally strong feelings about her, about this marriage working, about them sharing a life together. Convincing her of those feelings was his problem. Yet his perception told him she wasn't ready to come to terms with the marriage being real. It was easier for her to pretend nothing was happening. So be it. He wouldn't push. It wasn't his style, anyhow. There were other ways of insinuating himself into her life—subtly, almost unnoticeably—until perhaps they would become so involved she wouldn't even think of leaving him.

"Don't rush your decision," he said, ignoring her statement. "Give it some time and see how it goes."

Ken motioned the waiter over and they gave their orders. They talked during dinner about the people in the office she'd met that day, with Ken filling her in on years of gossip. They joked and laughed good-naturedly, a bond forming between them.

As Janet listened to Ken describe one of the office worker's antics at last year's Christmas party, she realized that he would be a good friend. Every minute of every day, a new facet of his personality was revealed to her. She had to admit, she liked what she saw. She more than liked it.

As the waiter served coffee, a mellowness settled over them. They were relaxed, enjoying each other's company—almost like any other newlywed couple....

"Peter called last night," Janet said, more to break her train of thought than to make conversation.

"How's he doing?" Ken asked.

"He's looking forward to his visit with us. He's a little nervous about it. I guess I am, too."

"Don't be. We'll make some plans to take him around the city. I have a town house on the east side. We can do whatever he wants."

"That's very nice of you to offer, Ken, but you really don't have to entertain him."

"I know I don't have to. I want to." He shook his head at her. "Don't be a party pooper. The kid's been locked up in that mausoleum for three months! Give him a break. We'll show him the town." He nudged her arm playfully. "Come on, say yes."

He was impossible to resist when he turned on the charm, and her face reflected the depth of her feelings for him. "Yes," she whispered.

Ken's breath caught at the changes he saw taking place in her eyes. He was getting to her; he could feel it. It was so difficult to control his emotions, but it was more important he did so now than ever before. He wanted her, not only physically, though God knew the ache inside wouldn't subside; he also wanted her heart, her soul, her thoughts. How had this happened to him? he wondered.

He brought her hand to his mouth and kissed the palm. "Dance with me?"

Janet nodded, mesmerized by the look in his eyes and the heat of his touch. They rose and walked the short distance to the lounge dance floor. They gently swayed in unison to the haunting melody.

Ken held her close and she rested her head on his chest, breathing in his scent, feeling warm, secure, wanted. They continued to dance into the next set, not speaking, neither wishing to break the mood. She gently rubbed her body against his, savoring the feel of him.

"Excuse me? Mr. Radnor?"

Ken stopped and turned to see their waiter standing nearby.

"Yes?"

"A phone call, sir. You can take it by the entrance."

"Who knows I'm here?" he asked Janet.

"Brian does. He recommended the restaurant."

"I wonder what's wrong."

Janet broke away from him. "There's only one way to find out," she said, pointing to the doorway.

Ken nodded. "I'll be right back."

Janet returned to the table and took a sip of wine.

"Hello."

She looked up at the sound of the masculine voice and recognized Doug Carmichael immediately.

"Mr. Carmichael! What a pleasant surprise! Please join us."

Doug didn't sit, but continued to hover over her.

"I don't think so, Janet. Is it okay if I call you that?" He continued after she nodded. "I don't think your husband would appreciate the intrusion. I would like to speak to *you*, however. Do you think we could have lunch sometime?''

"Mr. Carmichael—"

"'Doug.'"

"Doug . . . I assume you mean lunch without my husband's knowledge. And I have to tell you, that's out of the question."

"If you tell any of the Radnors, they won't allow you to meet with me. Believe me, I've tried for years to get a meeting with them—it's been a losing battle."

"First of all," Janet began, "if I felt the need to meet with you, I would, with or without the Radnors' blessings, but frankly, Doug, I don't see what you could possibly have to say to interest me."

"I have a proposition for the Radnor family that will help not only them, but you, too. There's a lot you don't know about them. They need capital right now. I have it and am willing to invest in Radnor Corporation. It would solve a lot of problems and right a long-standing wrong, as well."

"What wrong?"

"Have lunch with me," he said with a grin, "and I'll tell you the whole story."

He was persuasive, and his offer of knowledge about the Radnors very appealing. Janet felt herself being swayed.

"I don't know. I really don't see what I could do."

"You have a seat on their board. Give me one hour, and I'll tell you."

"Why don't you sit down, and we'll talk this over with Ken. Here he comes now."

Ken returned to the table.

"Was that your idea of a joke, Carmichael?" Ken's hand was clenched, and to say he was angry would be an understatement.

"I needed a minute with your lovely bride, Ken, without you protecting her like a mama bear with her cub."

"What do you want?" Ken demanded.

Carmichael straightened his large frame to its full height and stood face-to-face with Ken.

"The same thing I've wanted for the past five years."

"No one's interested, Douglas, least of all my wife."

The two men stared at each other with grim expressions, their eyes locked in some private battle.

"I've said my hellos, now I'll say my goodbyes." Doug turned back to Janet. "Mrs. Radnor, always a pleasure to see you." He leaned over and took her hand, placing a brief kiss on the back as he mumbled, "I'll call you."

Doug left, a sardonic look on his face that irked Ken to no end.

"What did he want?"

"Why does he make you so angry? He's really very charming."

"About as charming as a viper in a bird's nest. What did he want with you?"

Janet was put off by his obvious hostility. What was between these two? Confused and unsure, she played safe. "Nothing. He just stopped by to say hello."

"Well, there was no phone call. Your 'charming' Doug likes to play games. Remember that."

Janet didn't like his arrogant attitude, especially with her. She hadn't done anything wrong!

"Yes, sir, I'll be sure to do that!" She rose and picked up her purse. "I think the evening is officially over."

She walked out of the restaurant, leaving Ken to settle the bill.

The air was thick with silence during the ride home. Janet and Ken were both lost in thought. Everything had been going so well, she couldn't understand how it all collapsed in a matter of minutes. What was it about Doug Carmichael that set Ken off that way? Ken claimed he was after her stock, yet he'd never mentioned it. Was the stock so important to Ken that it took precedence over all other things in his life? Even her? She wondered what Doug's "proposition" was.

"What is it with you two, anyway?" she asked.

Ken didn't answer right away, and she noticed that his jaw was clenched. Whatever it was, the feeling ran deep. Just when she thought he wasn't going to answer, he spoke.

"Douglas Carmichael and I go way back. We went to school together. And while I'll admit I was the first one to sling mud, we've been at each other's throats for years."

"What happened to start it off?"

Ken related the episode at the country club snack bar when they were teenagers. "And since that day, it's gotten worse, with each one of us always scheming to get back at the other."

"It seems rather childish to me."

"I agree. Or at least it was—until five years ago."

"When your father died?"

"Yes. Dad had been working for months on a bid to buy out a company by the name of Bradford, Ltd. He spent every waking moment on the project. He wanted to expand and Bradford fitted right into his plans. It was the culmination of all he'd worked for."

"What does Doug have to do with this?"

"Everything. He outbid us. The amount was small enough to convince us he had a spy in our organization. He had to have. He couldn't have come that close without some inside information. My father never recovered from the blow. He died within two weeks of losing the bid."

"And you blame Doug for it."

"Yes. We all did. It wasn't so much that he outbid us, as the fact that he was underhanded about it. We could never prove a thing, so we had to lay it to rest. The worst part was that my father gave him his start. Without Gil Radnor, Douglas Carmichael would be working in a factory somewhere, probably drunk as a skunk most of the time like his old man." Ken made the turn into the driveway and stopped the car in front of the house. "That was the thanks my father received. A knife in the back at a time in his life when he should have been on top of the world."

Ken turned in his seat to look at her. "Now do you understand why my family can't—and won't—do business with Douglas Carmichael?"

"I understand how you feel, yes," Janet said. "But it's been five years. Don't you think you should at least give him a chance to explain?"

"Explain what? How he did it? No thank you. I have no wish to listen to any of his lies. And neither should you. Stay away from him, Janet. I'm not open to negotiation on this one."

Janet bristled under his autocratic tone, but understood that this was more than a sore point with him. "I'll think about it," she said as they emerged from the car.

Ken slammed the car door and leaned over the low-slung hood of the car to stare across at her. "Don't fight me on this, Janet. There's no halfway here. It's either me or him."

"And you don't threaten me," she said, her anger rising to the surface. "None of this has anything to do with me."

"You're my wife."

"Temporarily."

Ken was stunned by her reply. Janet wished she could bite back the word as soon as it had left her mouth. She could tell by the look on his face, but it was too late now. He walked away from the car with stone-cold precision, effectively putting his back to her, and climbed the stairs to the front door, which he opened and disappeared behind.

Janet wrapped her arms around herself to ward off the cold. "So much for 'dessert,'" she said to the empty night.

Janet entered the rooms she shared with Ken, and knew he hadn't returned to them. She supposed he planned to spend the night in Brian's suite. She leaned against the closed door and shut her eyes tightly, wincing in frustration. She knew she could have handled things better, but the thought brought little comfort.

Something had to be done. All day long thoughts of what the night would bring had whirled through her head. When Ken had kissed her in his office, the promise of more to come had been alive, and had grown stronger throughout dinner. He'd told her that the business had nothing to do with their personal feelings. Yet he was ignoring his desires and allowing the business to take over. The ache of that unfulfilled promise burned within her and wouldn't subside.

Having had no experience with suppressing sexual desire, she felt like a child denied a much-wanted candy bar. She wanted him. It was that plain and simple.

And she would have him.

Janet pushed herself away from the door and, with a determined stride, made her way into the bedroom. Pulling open the dresser drawer, she rummaged through its contents until she came up with her choice. Grinning, she threw the flimsy negligee onto the bed and began to undress. The silken material glided down her body as she slipped it over her head. The pale peach color complimented the honey of her hair, and she pulled out the pins to let the tresses fall down her back. She brushed it with long strokes until her hair gleamed in the evening light. After lightly touching up her makeup, she was ready.

Janet stepped back to examine herself in the full-length mirror. Her face was flushed and her hair framed her face with sweeping, cascading waves. Because of its color, her nightgown appeared practically transparent, but the sheer material of the floral appliqué that decorated the bust line was virtually flesh tone. Suspended by two thin straps, the gown was form-fitting and hugged her figure. Janet had questioned herself when she'd bought it, but now she knew why she had.

She'd been planning this all along.

Before reaching the door, she hesitated, wondering if she should wear a robe. Brazenly she decided against it, and opening the door, she stepped out into the hallway. It was deserted, and she breathed a sigh of relief. She padded down the long corridor in bare feet, rounding the corner to what she hoped was the door to Brian's rooms. When she arrived, she stopped dead. Her heart was beating triple time, and she was sure she would never carry this off. Her palms were damp and the flush of her face made her skin tingle. She wiped her hands down the sides of the gown, closed her eyes and breathed deeply before knocking.

"Hell-o, hell-o! What have we here?"

It was Brian, and she was totally unprepared to deal with him. Her mouth hung open as she tried to scan the room behind him.

"Looking for someone, Janet?" he teased. "Now let me see. Could it be Eleanor? Edmund, then. No? Well, who, I wonder?"

"Brian, please. Is Ken here?"

Brian's eyes twinkled mischievously, but he seemed to hesitate and bite his tongue.

"Come on in. He's in the shower. I'll get him."

Janet walked into the room, mortified at being caught by Brian. She assumed he would be out. He was *always* out. Why on earth was he home early tonight of all nights? She was in the middle of arguing with herself, when Ken walked into the room, still dripping under his navy terrycloth robe.

"Janet." He tipped his head as he rubbed his hair with a towel. "Is something wrong?" She could tell he was still angry, but was hiding it for the benefit of his brother.

"No," she said awkwardly, "nothing's wrong. I just wanted to . . . well, you know . . ."

It was at that moment that Ken gave her his full attention and realized what she was wearing. She noticed his face turn first white, then quickly red. He glanced back at Brian, who was lounging against the couch, thoroughly enjoying the show. Ken turned back to her, fire in his eyes.

"What, Janet? You wanted to what?"

"Talk. I wanted to talk to you."

"I think you've said enough for tonight, don't you?"

"I—"

Both Ken and Janet looked at Brian.

"Don't mind me," Brian said innocently.

Ken grabbed her arm and headed for the door. "Come on." He ushered her down the hall, trying his best to ignore Brian's diminishing chuckle as he guided her back to his own apartment. Once inside, he shut the door and leaned against it. "What was the idea behind this one, Janet?"

She fidgeted as she walked away from him, putting the sofa between them. "I told you."

"Oh, yes! You wanted to talk. So you parade around the house half-naked in front of my brother, just to talk to me."

"I didn't parade around! And I'm not half-naked, either!"

"No? How would you describe that . . . that—?"

"Ken, please, don't do this, don't ruin . . ."

He walked toward her, then stopped, his stance less threatening than before.

"Ruin what?" he asked softly.

She looked up at him, her heart in her eyes. "Everything."

Ken took the few steps between them and pulled her into his arms, claiming her mouth completely. Her lips were soft, warm, and her body so inviting. He reached down and cupped her buttocks, molding her to him, as his tongue and lips continued their assault.

But he broke away, his body ready, his mind in turmoil. She'd said "temporarily." Did that mean she wanted him physically with no commitment, nothing else involved?

"Woman," he growled into her ear. "What is it you want from me?"

Janet lightly scratched her fingernails along his jaw, down his neck, then insinuated her hands into the folds of his robe to caress the thick matted hair on his chest. This was what she wanted; but not only this, more, all he had to give.

She reached up and outlined the shell of his ear with her tongue and she whispered the answer to his question. "Dessert."

Ken stilled. She could feel the pounding of his heart beneath her hand and she knew her request was taking a minute to cleave the cloud of desire inside his head. When he finally looked down at her, his eyes were wild, the primitive male ready to mate, and she reveled in what she saw.

All questions and rational thought vanished from his mind. As he scooped her into his arms and carried her toward the bedroom, the sound he made was almost violent. The look in her eyes foretold of the passion to come. Ken was drowning in their depths, her gaze tugging at him, reeling him in. He rested her gently on the bed and sat back, savoring the moment. She lay quietly, returning his look, seemingly content for him to make the first move. His blood was pounding in his ears. He'd never been this aroused. Everything before paled in comparison. The dreams of the day were about to be fulfilled, and he suppressed the need to rush. He wanted to take his time with her, make love leisurely, lovingly, lastingly. He wanted to create a memory.

As much as he loved the nightgown, it had to go. In a swift motion, he helped her remove it, and his robe quickly followed. He lay down beside her on the bed, supporting himself on an elbow as he reacquainted himself with the contours of her body. He marveled at the creaminess of her skin. They didn't speak as the crescent-shaped moon cast a shimmer of light across the bed. They didn't have to; their bodies were doing the talking for them.

Janet was supersensitive to his touch. It seemed as if all her nerve endings were electrified. She reached out to feel the taut skin on his arms and shoulders. They explored each other in the semidarkness, until all at once it was too much, not enough.

He kissed her. Softly at first, then with more urgency, demanding all she had to give, and she gave it willingly. His lips and teeth played with her until she opened her mouth for him and he gratefully accepted the invitation. His tongue touched hers slowly, sensuously, foretelling of things to come. He slid his mouth down her neck to her special pulse point, then beyond, to the glory of her breasts. He kissed them, suckled first one, then the other, his mouth wet, hot, thorough. Janet's body rocked with the onslaught of feelings he aroused. She moaned slightly as he pressed kisses to her abdomen, then the smooth skin of her thighs. Her legs tensed, then relaxed as he nuzzled her thick, golden curls before looking up at her love-dazed eyes.

She thought she heard him murmur something about dessert before she became lost in sensation.

And then she heard nothing. He worked such magic she needed to grip the sheets to keep from crying out. But eventually she couldn't hold back any longer. Her moan began in the very recesses of her soul and inched its way up, tentatively at first, until it was full-blown, vocal, immediate. She ran her fingers over his shoulders and through his hair, pulling and pushing at him simultaneously. Then all of a sudden she arched against him, dancing to the sparkling lights that filled her head, and she closed her eyes tightly in an effort to control the tremors that racked her body.

She opened her eyes to see a tousle-haired Ken smiling down at her. She blinked to clear her vision. He was thoroughly pleased with himself—as well he should be, she supposed—but they weren't finished yet.

Not by a long shot.

Much later, they lay side by side, barely touching. Ken's arms were folded under his head, and he stared at the ceiling in silent wonder. His feelings for her ran deep and the fact that they'd only known each other a short time didn't lessen the sense of desolation her flip remark about the nature of their relationship had created. He wanted her to know how he felt, but his pride refused to let her see how much it had affected him.

Janet reached out and caressed his chest. To say that what they had just shared was beautiful would have been inadequate. They were truly one with the other, and nothing or no one could alter that fact. She knew she was fighting a losing battle, keeping him at arm's length. It had been too late for that since the first time they'd made love. She was learning so much about herself, her own sensuality, which had been locked away for so long, that it frightened her. *He* frightened her. Was she truly sabotaging the relationship, as he'd said?

Ken took hold of her hand on his chest and stilled its movements. He held it tightly for a moment, then took a deep breath and turned his body toward her. Their eyes met and held in the darkness. He studied her face and she smiled, but he didn't return it.

"You're wrong, you know," he whispered. "There's nothing temporary about this."

She touched her lips to his, "I know," she said, as she rolled her body on top of him. "I know."

Eleven

————

She wished she knew if she was doing the right thing.

Janet sat in her car in the parking lot of Harry's Pub. It was noon, and this was the time and place Doug Carmichael had asked her to meet him. When he'd originally called, she'd had no intention of showing up at all. As much as her curiosity was piqued, she had no desire to go against Ken's wishes and meet with his rival. But as it turned out, Ken had canceled their plans for lunch today, as he had an important meeting with their new banker, leaving her at loose ends. He'd seemed preoccupied, but unwilling to talk, so she hadn't pursued it. Were the Radnors having serious money problems as Doug had hinted? Impulsively she'd grabbed her purse and headed for the restaurant.

But now that she was here, all those doubts resurfaced. Ken would be furious if he knew. His mind was closed to any discussion on Douglas Carmichael. Based on what he'd told her about what happened with his father, she felt he had every reason to dislike and distrust Doug—that is, if it was all true. Her instincts supported a nagging suspicion that Ken didn't have the whole story. Could she get to the bottom of it?

The weekend spent with Peter had been a success. They'd stayed overnight at Ken's town house in New York, seeing a play and a hockey game. On Sunday afternoon, Ken and Peter had left her to shop Fifth Avenue while they'd gone across the river to New Jersey to a football game. They'd returned fast friends, and it had warmed her heart to see Peter relate so well to another man.

In the weeks since, the Radnors had celebrated a quiet, traditional family Thanksgiving. But she and Ken had shared an uneasy truce since that night they'd met Doug in the restaurant. No one noticed, except her. Ken was kind, polite and certainly went out of his way with Peter; but there was also a remoteness, a wall that had descended. She knew he was protecting himself by putting up barriers to ward off his feelings for her. Her insensitive remark about their marriage being only temporary was the cause, and she wished she could go back in time and swallow the word before it had emerged. She'd blown it, and try as she might, she couldn't coax back that open and carefree Ken she'd come to love.

Something had to be done. But was meeting Carmichael only adding fuel to an already-smoldering fire? Janet sighed. Her choice had already been made the minute she'd entered the car. She felt compelled to meet with him, to know what he knew about the Radnors, to make her feel more a part of what was going on—to help, if she was able, end this feud. She slammed the car door a little harder than necessary and headed for the entrance. The hostess requested her name, then immediately led her to a table in the corner of the dining room.

"Thank you for coming."

Douglas was impeccably groomed. His three-piece navy suit was custom-tailored. The white shirt and navy-and-gray striped tie complemented his auburn hair and ruddy complexion. He looked every bit the powerful executive and—judging by the stolen looks from the other women in the restaurant—every bit an attractive male.

"I must say," he continued, "I'm surprised you're here. I thought Radnor would stop you."

"He's my husband, not my owner," she said as she sat in the chair he held for her. "I can do as I please." She didn't add that Ken didn't know.

"I hope that's true, because you're my last hope. I need your help, Janet."

"What is this all about, Doug?"

"It's not the stock, if that's what you're thinking. Although *because* of the stock, you're in a position to do me a great service."

Janet opened her mouth to speak, but was preempted.

"Before you say anything, let me tell you that I know about the conditions of your marriage. In spite of—or maybe because of it—you're in a unique situation. It gives you board voting rights. That's where I need your help."

"How did you find out about my marriage agreement?"

Doug shrugged. "Gossip, rumors. Once heard, it was easy to get to the bottom of it. I cornered Paul Bradly at the wedding and he filled me in on the details."

"I don't think I like the idea of being run through the rumor mill."

"Don't knock it," Doug said, grinning. "Gossip is a very powerful—and popular, I might add—weapon in business. It's used all the time."

"But rumors aren't always true."

"There's always a grain of truth in them. They usually lead you in the right direction, anyway."

"Then maybe you can clear up some rumors I've heard about you," she asked.

Doug laughed. "Fire away."

"Is it true you betrayed Ken's father?"

Janet watched the big man sit back in his chair. His jacket opened with the motion, revealing a massive chest, yet he was graceful, practiced in his movements, so that one didn't dwell on how large he was, only how powerful. He was studying her as if she were under a microscope, and she sensed he was trying to determine how much to reveal about himself. She noticed his eyes squint and chin lift slightly.

"Have you ever been on the outside looking in, Janet?"

Janet remembered all those years in orphanages and foster homes, feeling alone, unwanted. The thought drew a solemn cloud across her eyes. "Yes. I have," she answered, returning his deep gaze.

"Then you know how I felt growing up in this town, where the Radnors were kings. I was always pushing, running toward something—what, I didn't know. Until I graduated college and formed my first company. Then I felt the power of being in charge, being one of *them*. I liked the feeling. And as youth will do, I went about righting all the wrongs I thought had been perpetrated against me." He reached into his jacket pocket and withdrew a pack of cigarettes. "Do you mind?" When she shook her head, he lit a cigarette, then continued, "The Radnor boys were the first on my hit list, of course. They'd always been so condescending when I was growing up. Especially Ken. I must say, he and I have always shared a love-hate relationship." He blew out a stream of smoke. "Well, anyway, to get to the point, I pulled some quick—and I'll brag and also say shrewd—business deals out from under the Radnors' noses. That didn't go down well, to say the least, but it *did* make them sit up and take notice."

"Ken mentioned all of this. I told him and I'll tell you— it all seems rather juvenile to me."

"No doubt it is. Don't you know that men are just little boys in disguise and instead of toys, they fight over money and power?"

"Ken becomes irrational about anything you're involved in. There's more to it than childish pranks."

"Well, Ken and Brian—Edmund, too—sometimes have a warped sense of things. They only recognize wrongs done to them. They think I had something to do with their father's death."

"Did you?"

Doug crushed out the cigarette. "No. Gil Radnor was the only one in the family who treated me as a human being. He was my mentor, a father figure, someone whom I respected more than anyone else in the world. He gave me my start and helped me grow. I'll admit that I did buy out a company—Bradford, Ltd.—he'd had his eye on for years. But that was part of a plan, and he knew about it. Gil had a heart attack soon after that, and they all blamed it on me. Believe me when I tell you, I had nothing to do with it."

"But Ken thinks you did."

Doug stared at her. "Yes."

"And now he thinks you want to sit on his board of directors."

"Yes."

"And you want me to help you do that."

"Yes."

"Why should I betray my husband? Give me one good reason."

Janet watched as he leaned forward, elbows on the table. The waiter interrupted at that time and took their orders.

"I don't look at it as betrayal," Doug said after he'd departed. "The Radnors are cash poor right now. They've reinvested most of their capital in new equipment for one of their companies. But you know that much, don't you? What you may not know is that they've got a huge balloon payment due soon. I happen to have a surplus of capital, and want to buy into Radnor Corporation. I want to bring Bradford into the corporation, as well. That, in a nutshell, is the plan I want you to help me with."

"I don't see how I can do any of this for you. Edmund barely speaks to me, and the only end of the business I'm familiar with now is in office administration."

"Janet, you're the first Radnor in five years even to agree to talk to me. Believe me when I tell you that you have a tremendous amount of power in that family. You own stock. You're on the board of directors. You can call a special meeting at any time."

"That's what you want me to do? Call a meeting?"

"Yes."

"And say what?" Janet shook her head. "Doug, there's no way I can do this. I'm not prepared to handle this type of business deal."

"I'll have it all worked out for you. You'll only have to make the presentation. You don't even have to tell them it's from me." He paused. "This is a good deal, Janet. Good for the Radnors, for me certainly, and for you, too."

"I don't see what I get out of all of this."

"Don't you? You get your freedom—if you want it."

Janet turned her head. How could she tell this man she didn't *want* to be free, without really telling him? Her hesitation spoke volumes, however.

"So that's the way it is! You're in love with Ken, aren't you?" There was something akin to awe in his voice.

"Doug—"

"Don't deny it. It's written all over your face." His own split into a grin. "So much the better. Does Ken feel the same way about you?"

"I really don't see what this has to do with anything."

Doug straightened in his seat. "It doesn't. It just might make things easier, that's all. Gil would have been happy. He always wanted to see Ken settled."

"You seem to know a lot about what Gil Radnor wanted," Janet said.

Doug sat back and accepted the luncheon dish from the waiter, studying Janet as they were served. It seemed to her as if he were holding something in, something important.

"Gil and I were very close. My own father was the town drunk, and if Gil hadn't taken an interest in me, I don't know where I'd have ended up. Our relationship caused some problems with his own sons, but that never stopped him. He always found a way to include me without offending them. I *know* that he would have wanted this deal to go through."

"So you say," Janet said. "But according to the Radnors, their father was very adamant about not having anyone outside the family sit on their board of directors. How do you explain that away?"

"I don't have to. The deal will stand on its own, Janet. They would be fools to turn it down, and believe me, if my name's not mentioned, they'll jump at the chance."

They ate their lunch in silence. Janet was deep in thought. Doug had made a lot of good points. If the Radnors needed money, here was a perfect opportunity for them to get a good, solid investor. It also meant they could actually pay for her stock. This was the most tempting part of the offer as far as she was concerned. If this block of stock was gone from their lives, she and Ken could truly start a relationship based on love, not on money.

"Well, Janet?" Doug asked as coffee was being served.

"I don't know. I'll have to think about it."

Doug nodded. "Please do."

He reached behind his seat and lifted his briefcase onto his lap. Opening it, he extracted a manila folder and handed it to her. "I'd like you to look this over. It's a complete copy of the proposal. It's a sound offer, Janet, and something I've wanted for a long time. It's what Gil wanted, too."

"So you said before. I wish there were a way to prove that to Ken."

Doug's eyes wandered toward the picture window of the restaurant. He seemed about to say something, but thought better of it. The waiter came and he paid the bill.

Janet stood, and he took her hand.

"Thank you again for coming today. Think about what I've said. It can work out for all of us."

He walked her to the parking lot and saw her to her car.

"Here's my card," he said. "As soon as you decide, call me. Even if it's over the weekend."

Janet laughed out loud. "Nothing like a little pressure, Mr. Carmichael!"

Doug had the good grace to look embarrassed. "Force of habit," he said. "Take all the time you need. I've waited this long, a few weeks one way or the other won't matter."

He shut the car door and leaned over to talk to her as she rolled down the window.

"Will you and Ken be going to the country club Christmas party?"

Janet nodded. "Yes, I'm told the Radnors are one of the sponsors of the charity affair. They always take a table."

"I'll see you there. Perhaps you'll have made your decision by then."

Janet watched him walk away. For some strange reason, she liked and trusted Douglas Carmichael. He and Ken should be friends, not enemies. On the seat next to her lay the folder. She stared at it, deep in thought. A tiny spark of excitement rippled at the idea of calling a board meeting herself and making this proposal. Could she do it? She didn't know, but if it meant an end to this madness between the two men, it might be worth a try.

Twelve

Janet's fingers were shaking. The tiny post of her diamond earring wouldn't go through her ear no matter how slowly and delicately she attempted the maneuver. She angled her head at the mirror to allow the best view, but she still couldn't see what she was doing. Her hands were beginning to perspire and her nerves were frazzled.

Since her luncheon with Douglas Carmichael, her mind had replayed his words and the doubts that tagged along. Should she get involved in this? It wasn't any of her business, yet she felt as if she were being inexplicably drawn into a tempest. Could any good come out of her involvement? Doug seemed to think so. She wished she were as sure.

Still, she found herself rehearsing how she would present the proposal at a meeting. The offer was as direct and straightforward as Doug had said. It *was* a good, solid offer, and it made sense. Even with her limited business expertise, she could see that. What she needed to do was generate some interest with the Radnor men before calling the meeting. She dared not approach Ken as yet, and Edmund was out of the question. That left Brian as her only rational hope. He'd been out of town all week. She needed to corner him this evening at the party to solicit his support.

That, weak as it seemed, was her plan. It wasn't the best but until inspiration hit it was all that she had.

She observed Ken's reflection in the mirror as he moved around the bedroom behind her. He was already dressed in a formal white pleated shirt, complete with black onyx studs which, no doubt *he'd* had no trouble fastening. A black satin cummerbund was fitted around his waist, matching the stripe down each pant leg. The black satin bow tie was secured and in place, perfectly straight and centered. All he needed to do was put on the jacket and he would be ready.

Perfectly ready, she thought, as she gave up on the earring and picked up her loose powder brush to pat the sheen on her nose. He looked so handsome in the tuxedo. It complemented his dark good looks and tall, hard frame. He looked like an ad for Bill Blass, and she wanted to touch him so badly it hurt.

She willed him to scream at her, holler or rage; this polite indifference was killing her! She loved him, but to tell him now would seem insincere and placating, even to her own ears.

He turned and their eyes met in the mirror.

"Are you almost ready?" Ken asked.

Janet turned on the stool in front of the vanity, her pale blue robe parting to show an expanse of leg. It wasn't a conscious gesture on her part, but she made no attempt to cover herself. Ken stared for a heavy moment, then looked away.

Janet sighed. "Almost. I only have to put my dress on." She turned back toward the vanity tray. "And get these damn earrings through my ears!"

He walked toward her so quietly she didn't realize he was behind her until his reflection filled the mirror.

"Can I help?" he asked softly.

She looked up at him, her eyes filled with want. "Please..."

Ken put out his hand and she dropped the earring and post into his palm. He studied the pieces for a moment, then knelt beside her. "Turn your head."

He leaned over her and worked on inserting the earring. He was so close, his breath fanned her hair. If she felt warm before, it was nothing compared to the heat that was rising between them now. It had been only a few days since they'd made love, but it seemed like years. Her body hungered for him and her pulse quickened. His fingers on her neck and ear seared like a brand.

"There," he said.

She turned her head and their eyes met. She recognized the longing she saw, and knew he wanted to kiss her. She wanted him to kiss her. He reached toward her cheek, and she instinctively parted her lips in anticipation. But instead of a kiss, he tilted her head in the other direction.

"Where's the other one?" he asked.

Disappointed, Janet handed him the diamond.

He quickly and efficiently finished the job and stood, "There. All done. I'll wait for you in the other room."

"Thank you," she said to his retreating back.

She admonished her image in the mirror. Fool! He wasn't going to fall at her feet, just because she wanted him to! She squared her jaw and lifted her chin. *Okay, Mr.*

Radnor, you need convincing, I'll convince you! The time for petty quarrels is over, for me as well as Doug Carmichael.

She entered the walk-in closet and picked out the cocktail dress she'd bought during her Fifth Avenue shopping spree. The dress fitted to perfection. She examined herself in the full-length mirror on the closet door. The black velvet bodice was snug, highlighting her full bosom with a delicate and tasteful décolleté. The shimmering teal-blue taffeta skirt fell almost to her ankles and the black *peau-de-soie* heels added to her graceful height. Her hair was pulled up in an artfully haphazard design the beautician had labored over for hours that day, expertly braiding in a black satin clip as a focal point.

Janet drew one of the full-length black gloves onto her left hand and arm. She picked up a thin diamond bracelet to secure it on her wrist before sliding her right hand into the other glove. One final look, and she was ready. Picking up her mink coat from the bed, she draped it over her arm and headed for the next room to meet Ken.

"I'm ready," she said to his back as she entered the room.

Ken turned, and for a brief moment, she thought his eyes would pop out of his head.

"You're not going anywhere in that dress."

Like a threatened cat, her back went up.

"What's wrong with this dress?"

"Nothing's wrong with it—here in this room. But you're not going outside with it on. What the hell's holding it up, for pete's sake?"

"Me."

"That's what I was afraid of. I'll wait while you change."

"I'm not changing."

"You're not going with me dressed like that."

"Then I'll go alone."

Janet walked toward the door.

"Janet..." he warned.

She stopped. "What?"

"You must have something else in that closet to wear."

Janet put her hand on her hip in defiance, her blue eyes on fire. He marveled at how she could change from sweet and innocent to hellfire and brimstone at the drop of a hat. She never looked so beautiful to him as she did now. His blood was racing, and all he wanted to do was tug on the top of that dress and release her breasts into his hands. Why was it the more angry she made him, the more he wanted her?

"Yes, I do have something else in my closet, but I'm not going to wear it. I'm wearing this dress. It's perfectly respectable, very much in style and cost me a small fortune. Everyone is wearing strapless dresses, and I don't see why I can't."

"You're my wife," he said softly.

Janet took a deep breath and fought the tears those simple words brought to her eyes. "Am I?"

It was a loaded question that, at the moment, he was unprepared to answer. He stared her down for what seemed like an eternity, but she wouldn't look away. He knew a lost cause when he saw one and took hold of her elbow.

"Let's go."

They rode to the party in angry silence. In a way, Ken knew he was being deliberately difficult, but he couldn't help himself. The dress, while it bothered him to see her in public like that, was only a smoke screen for what had been building inside of him all week. He was still smarting from her callous remark. But more than that, he felt totally powerless with her. He loved her, but he was used to getting what he wanted when he wanted it. With Janet, things never seemed to work out as smoothly. She defied him, and while he admired her spunk, he hated the lack of control. Her attitude toward Carmichael was a prime example. She hadn't mentioned it again, but he knew the matter wasn't settled. Doug would be there tonight. Would he seek her out? If he did, would she be receptive?

Janet chewed on her lip, deep in thought. She needed to find Brian as soon as they arrived. He, at least, would be reasonable. She turned her head toward Ken and studied his granite profile. *I love you,* she told him silently. Sighing, she looked out the passenger window. She prayed to God she would find a way to work this out and make him believe that.

The main ballroom of the country club was filled with women in brightly colored gowns, dripping with diamonds and jewels of every cut and color. The men looked prosperous in their tuxedos, and even the short and portly looked handsome in the formal attire. It was truly a gala event. Janet smiled broadly at the festive atmosphere and she noticed that even Ken's grim expression lightened when people greeted them as they made their way across the dance floor toward the Radnor family table.

A huge blue spruce Christmas tree was decorated in old-fashioned strings of popcorn and cranberries as well as lights made to look like candles. The band played familiar holiday standards and some of the older couples were dancing to the old favorites. Janet was introduced to several people she'd never met; she also reacquainted herself with many she'd been introduced to the day of their wedding.

"Janet," Ken said. "I'd like you to meet Lloyd and Sarah Wooley. Lloyd's our new banker over at First Federal."

"Hello," Janet said. "It's a pleasure to meet you both."

The Wooleys returned the greetings, and after a small amount of small talk, the men began discussing business. Janet nodded politely as Sarah Wooley began a steady stream of gossip about this one or that one, but she searched the room for Brian or Douglas or someone who would rescue her from the chattering woman.

"And you probably haven't met Libby Marshall yet— her husband is in securities, you know—but she told me that Lorraine Hutchins told her that..."

In the middle of all this, the light went off in her head. *Gossip.* Why hadn't she thought of that before? Hadn't Doug said it was a powerful weapon? Well, it could also be a powerful tool.

"Mrs. Wooley," Janet interrupted, "your husband is one of the bankers our family does business with, isn't he?"

"Well, ah, yes, he is. As I was saying—"

"Then he must be the one who's handling our new acquisition," Janet said.

"Acquisition?"

"Yes, the new company Radnor is taking on. The one the new partner is bringing with him. I know you must have heard your husband talk about it. The influx of cash is so huge the bank must be very busy handling all the details."

"Well, of course, I'm sure they are. Did you say 'partner'? I don't remember anything about a new partner. I thought Radnor was always a family-owned business."

"Yes, that was the case in the past, but this new proposal was so innovative and exciting, the brothers couldn't pass it up. Sort of like an offer they couldn't refuse."

"I had no idea!" Mrs. Wooley's eyes were as big as saucers. "Shame on Lloyd for not telling me!"

"Oh, dear!" Janet covered her mouth with her hand in feigned chagrin. "I hope I haven't let the cat out of the bag! Ken will kill me! I thought everyone knew. Please don't say a word to anyone!"

Mrs. Wooley patted Janet's hand and smiled at the new bride. "Don't worry about a thing, dear. My lips are sealed. I haven't heard a word you said!"

"You're so kind," Janet said with a smile.

"Think nothing of it." Mrs. Wooley looked over Janet's shoulder. "Speak of the devil, there's Libby Marshall now. If you'll excuse me . . ."

"Certainly," Janet said, trying with all her might to control her grin. Well, if that didn't get the ball rolling, she didn't know what would.

Spotting Brian, she waved and walked across the room, leaving Ken deep in conversation with several men.

"Hello, Janet," Brian said as she took hold of his arm. "That's some dress!"

"Don't you start!"

"Start what? It looks great. Doesn't Ken like it?"

"He likes it fine, I'm told, but only in the bedroom."

Brian laughed. "Jealousy becomes him."

Janet shook her head. "I need to talk to you."

"What about?"

She hesitated, not knowing exactly how to begin. "I've been approached by someone with a very lucrative business proposal for Radnor Corporation. It would mean an enormous amount of money for the company, as well as a new acquisition. Interested?"

"Do I look dumb? Sure. Who made the offer?"

Janet stopped walking and faced him, looking him straight in the eyes. "Douglas Carmichael."

"Janet . . . forget it! You know how we feel about Carmichael!"

"Brian, please, have an open mind. Let me explain what he's offering, what he had to say. Certainly you must agree it's time to let bygones be bygones. This is business. And I think it's something your father would have wanted."

"You seem to know an awful lot about us in a short period of time, Janet."

"I'm learning. Will you give me a chance?"

"Let's find a table."

They walked to a sparsely occupied corner of the room and sat. Janet reviewed the key points of Douglas's proposal, including the Bradford merger. Brian's eyes were riveted to her, and she realized he wasn't all fun and games. The man, like the other Radnor brothers, had a brain.

"So you see," she concluded, "it would solve a lot of problems for the company. It will more than double your size and assets in one fell swoop."

"What you say makes sense, Janet, I'll admit that. I might even agree with you that we need something like this, but Doug Carmichael will be a hard sell."

"Then let's sell the package before we sell the man."

"You mean not tell Edmund and Ken who's behind the deal?"

Janet nodded. "First things first. Will you help me?"

Brian grinned. "What's in it for you?"

"Maybe a marriage."

Brian took her hand and squeezed it. "In that case, you've got my support. There's more to life than holding a grudge. I'll do whatever I can."

Janet hugged him. "You're the best."

They stood and were about to go their separate ways, when Brian grabbed hold of her arm. "So are you, Janet." He kissed her cheek. "Ken's a lucky guy."

Janet smiled as he walked away, then she went in search of Ken. She touched his shoulder to let him know she was back. Instinctively he drew an arm around her and brought her to his side. She leaned her head against him, and he looked away from the discussion long enough to see a dreamy expression on her face. He wanted more than anything to melt this wall of ice between them.

"Dance with me?" he asked.

She nodded and they excused themselves from the group and moved to the dance floor. Ken brought his arm around her and she rested her hand in his. They danced in silence, eye to eye as the band played a ballad. Ken's eyes were drawn to her cleavage, then roamed back to her face. Their eyes met. That smoldering fire that was always so close to the surface sparked between them.

"Let's go home," he said.

"But we just arrived!"

"I know. Let's leave, anyway."

He pulled her closer still, and their bodies began to move in tandem to the rhythm of the music.

"We can't leave now," she said. "And you know it."

"Then let's make up."

"You said you hated my dress."

"I don't hate it. I love it. It makes me nervous knowing this little thing—" he toyed with the zipper at the back of the dress "—is all that stands between you and total nudity."

She punched his shoulder playfully, happy his good mood was returning. "Stop that. It's perfectly safe and not going anywhere."

"For now," he said, his face breaking into a huge smile.

As always, that boyish transformation melted her heart. She shook her head at his antics and smiled back. He pulled her closer in response.

"Kenneth," Edmund said, with a tap on his shoulder. "Come away from here. I have to talk to you."

"Not now, Edmund. Can't you see we're dancing?"

"Dance later. I have to talk to you."

Edmund grabbed Ken's arm and pulled Janet along with him off the dance floor toward their table.

"Frank Marshall just cornered me. He didn't make a damn bit of sense, but the gist of it was that rumor has it we're involved in a major merger. Do you have any idea what he's talking about?"

Ken stared at his brother for a moment. "Merger? What merger?"

"Something about a new partner, huge amounts of money. I don't know."

"Where did he hear it from?"

"Wouldn't say. Then you're in the dark, too?" When Ken nodded, Edmund continued, "I'd better talk to Lloyd and get to the bottom of this."

Edmund left, and Ken turned to Janet, easing her back onto the dance floor. "I wonder what that was all about?" Janet shrugged. "Not that it wouldn't be a godsend if it was true," Ken continued.

Janet stopped dancing. "What did you say?"

He stared down at her. "Between you and me, sweetheart," he whispered, "we could use the cash."

Janet smiled broadly.

"You think that's funny?" Ken tilted his head in surprise at her reaction.

"No! Of course not!" she said with as much solemnity as she could muster.

The music stopped and they walked off the dance floor. Janet was elated at his reaction to the rumor. Her plan was working. Edmund was running from group to group, ferreting out information. She watched his eyes glitter with interest and knew she'd bagged him. Perhaps she *did* have a chance....

Douglas Carmichael walked into the ballroom. Janet felt Ken tense, and looked up at him, then followed his line of vision to the man coming toward them. Ken turned them around and began to walk in the other direction.

"Ken, please." Janet stopped and pulled away from him. "This is so childish. Can't we even be civil to him?"

"Go ahead, Janet, be as civil as you want. I'm sure you will be, anyway." He walked away.

Janet sighed, and her shoulders slumped in defeat. For a few minutes, she'd thought he might have come around....

"Hi."

Janet turned to Doug, a troubled look in her eyes. "Hello, Doug."

"Don't let it bother you," he said, indicating Ken's retreating back.

"I don't know how you stand it!"

Doug laughed. "Oh, I'm used to it. But I have faith in you. You're going to change all that."

"Don't count so heavily on me. I haven't the foggiest idea what I'm doing!"

"You've already made your decision."

Janet arched her eyebrows.

"I've heard the rumor," he said with a grin. "It's a beaut! Who'd you tell?"

"Sarah Wooley."

"Ha! That's as good as renting a megaphone and standing on the roof! Good girl!"

"I guess I'm in too deep to pull out now," she said.

Doug took her hand. "Call the meeting Monday, before you change your mind. If you need any help, get in touch with me tomorrow. And here." He handed her an envelope. "Read it tomorrow after you plan out your presentation. I'd rather you didn't use it unless your back is to the wall. Let the deal stand on its own. If it doesn't—" he waved the envelope in front of her "—use it."

She took it from him and put it in her bag. "What is it?"

"Tomorrow."

She nodded, and turned to see Ken approaching once again, a grim look on his face. She started toward him to ward off any confrontation.

"And, Janet..."

She glanced back at him.

"Thanks."

Janet smiled and gave him the thumbs-up sign. For better or for worse, she was committed.

Thirteen

Monday arrived all too soon as far as Janet was concerned. She checked her watch. It was almost time for the meeting to begin. She collated the remaining notes she'd made and placed them in the front of her folder. Ken had left for work very early in the morning for a special meeting with Edmund, so she'd driven to the office with Brian. She was grateful for the reprieve, because with her nerves as frazzled as they were, she wouldn't have been able to fool Ken for a moment. She'd practiced her presentation on Brian. He'd been extremely helpful in coordinating the meeting and reviewing the proposal. All was ready—as ready as it would ever be.

Janet took a deep breath and stood when Brian poked his head in the doorway.

"All set?" he asked.

"Yes," she answered. "Ken and Edmund agreed . . . ?"

"No problem. I told them we needed an impromptu meeting for you to make a presentation. They probably think it's something about the office staff."

Janet rolled her eyes. "I'll never pull this off!"

"Stop worrying. You'll be fine. You're well prepared. As I told you before, the key thing will be to convince Edmund *before* you mention Bradford. Don't harp on the money angle. Ed's more into prestige. Play to his ego. If we win Edmund over, it doesn't matter what Ken does. The two of them control the majority of the stock, but if we can split them, we've got a prayer."

"I know that."

She picked up the pile of folders and walked out of the office, Brian at her side. She stopped at the door to the board room and put her hand on his arm.

"It *is* a good deal, isn't it Brian?"

"Yes, it is. I like you, Janet, but I wouldn't be on your side if it wasn't also good for the company." He squeezed her arm. "Now go get 'em, tiger!"

Janet opened the door and walked inside the room. Edmund, Ken and a secretary were already present and seated around a rectangular table. Brian took a seat opposite Janet and gave her the thumbs-up sign. Edmund was at the head, with the secretary prepared to take notes at his right. Ken sat at the other end with a pad and pencil in front of him, seemingly engrossed in some figures. He looked up quickly and caught Janet's eye. She smiled tentatively, but he returned a big grin.

Ken rose from the table and walked over to her. He leaned down and she lifted her face to him. For a moment she thought he was going to kiss her, before realizing how ludicrous that would be considering where they were. Instead he whispered in her ear.

"What's this all about?"

"I—I was approached with a business proposal. I thought it wise to call a meeting right away."

"Who contacted you?" he asked.

There was no time to answer as Edmund called the board meeting to order. Ken gave her a puzzled look and reluctantly returned to his seat. Edmund covered some points he felt necessary and, soon after, abandoning parliamentary procedure, he confronted Janet.

"Now what the devil is this all about, Janet, that a board meeting had to be called?"

"I wanted to speak to all of you together about a proposal presented to me for Radnor Corporation."

"Couldn't we have talked about it at home, at dinner?" Edmund asked.

"No, I needed a more official setting, and in a moment, I think you'll see why." She took a deep breath and stood. "Gentlemen, I have here a proposition from a third party who wishes to make a very substantial investment in Radnor Corporation."

Edmund looked over at Ken. "This must have something to do with those rumors at the party Saturday night. Perhaps we'll get to the bottom of it."

Ken only nodded in response, casting a speculative look toward Janet, who pretended not to see as she continued.

"These are copies of the written proposal, which I'd like you to look at as I go over the main points," she said, passing out the folders.

"We're family owned, Janet. You know that. We've no interest in third-party investors. Who is this person, anyway?" Edmund demanded.

Janet handed him a folder and ignored his question as she continued.

"As you can see by the numbers involved, we're talking about a huge amount of capital." She caught Brian's eye and changed tactics. "An acceptance of this offer would virtually double Radnor's holdings, making us one of the largest corporations in the industry."

Edmund studied the first page. "Very impressive." He paused as he reviewed the figures. "This is a very interesting and lucrative offer. I'm curious, however. Why wasn't I contacted, or Kenneth, or Brian, for that matter? Why you, Janet?"

"I was most accessible at the time," she said smoothly.

Ken smiled, dropping his head so no one would see. The minute he looked at the proposal, he knew. Doug's handiwork was as familiar to him as his own. He'd felt the anger bubbling below the surface and was just about to explode and expose her, when he suppressed the urge and thought better of it. He wanted to see how she intended to get away with this.

He had to hand it to her. The proposal was professional, detailed and accurate regarding their situation. He shuddered to think of how she or Doug had obtained the information about Radnor finances. She was playing his brother like a master musician. Part of him couldn't help but be proud of her. He had to admit she had to have guts to face them all with this. He watched her parry and thrust with Edmund. His brother was a tough, shrewd businessman, but she was holding her own. Her facts were clear, concise and on target.

He realized something else, too, as he listened intently to her sales pitch. She was right. It was a solid offer that would be good for the company. He begrudgingly read through the proposal, following along with her as he mulled over the ramifications of accepting such a deal. It *did* make sense. It would solve a lot of their problems, both long- and short-term. Plus, they would take a quantum leap forward on their father's original master plan. The influx of money would enable them to implement programs that were years away in theory. They would be fools not to take the plunge.

If only Douglas Carmichael weren't involved...

He needed to give serious thought to this. What if Doug truly had nothing to do with his father's death? Was he only being unforgiving? Or just plain stubborn? He wished with all his might it had never come to this confrontation. He wished he'd taken Doug up on one of his many offers and handled this himself.

But that was water under the bridge. Ken needed to make up his mind, and quickly, whether he would give Doug the benefit of the doubt and back Janet on this. No matter how good her presentation was he knew that once Edmund heard about Doug, the game would be over. She needed him on her side or she would fail.

He watched his elder brother. Janet was doing very well. She had Edmund nearly salivating now that the entire picture was unfolding. The scenario of being president of a giant in the industry was too tempting, even for Edmund, with his strong belief in "family only," to resist. However, it was only a matter of time before Carmichael's name would have to be mentioned, and then, he knew, Edmund would explode.

"So you see, Edmund. This is a chance in a million, one that won't come along again, I'm sure. What do you say?"

Edmund looked up from the papers before him. "I'd be an idiot to say I'm not interested, Janet. Even my father, who never wanted any outsiders, would look at this offer seriously. But I'm still not clear on the merger. The assets involved are laid out here, but what company are we talking about?" he asked as he flipped through the folder. "I don't see where the name is mentioned."

Janet felt the perspiration trickle down between her breasts. The moment of reckoning was at hand. She looked at Brian and acknowledged his slight nod. She picked up the next set of folders and passed them around the table. "This will answer all your remaining questions, Edmund."

Edmund opened the first page, and everyone held his breath as his round face went to stark white, followed by a bright red glow that crept up from his neck to his hairline. The pulse point in his right temple began to throb and his collar all of a sudden seemed too tight around his throat. Janet froze as he began to sputter.

"Br-Bradford, Ltd.? My God! Douglas Carmichael! I can't believe you'd do this!" He glared at Janet. "Do you have any idea what this man has done to us?" he screamed.

"Get Ed a glass of water, please," Ken said to the secretary.

The woman quickly left the room as Ed pointed an accusing finger at all assembled.

"Did you all know about this?" He slammed his fist on the desk. "Did you?"

"Calm down," Brian said. "Don't let your emotions override your good sense. Look at the facts. Two minutes ago, you said it was a good deal and were champing at the bit. The deal hasn't changed."

"Oh, yes, it has!" Edmund roared. "I suppose you've forgotten what he's done now that you're so willing to do business with him. You are, aren't you, Brian? You're with her in this! Well, I'm not! I won't do business with a thief and a scoundrel!"

"Douglas Carmichael is neither," Janet said.

"You know nothing about this, young lady! All you've caused is trouble to me and my family. How dare you defend that man to me!"

"Take it easy, Edmund," Ken said, indicating the glass of water that had been placed in front of him. "Take a drink before you pass out."

Edmund obeyed and sipped the water, glaring at his brothers and Janet over the rim of the glass.

"And where do *you* stand on this, Kenneth?"

All eyes turned to Ken. He felt Janet's most of all as he looked at her and saw her heart in her eyes. He swallowed and said a quick prayer that he was doing the right thing.

"It's a good deal, Ed. We need the money. And you're right. Even Dad wouldn't pass this up. I think we should go with it."

Janet sank into her seat, awash with a mixture of emotions: pride in Ken's ability to overcome his own prejudice, gratitude for his support of her in front of his beloved brother... and love, overwhelming and complete love for this man who was truly her partner, her friend, her husband.

Their eyes met and held, communicating the million things they couldn't say to each other out loud in this place, saying the one thing they'd never said to each other at all—"I love you."

"So, I'm outnumbered, am I?" Edmund said, his color returning to normal. "I can't believe this! My own flesh and blood siding against me with a man who was instrumental in our father's death, a man who spied, stole, connived—"

"He did none of those things," Janet interrupted.

"Janet. Don't tell me what he has or hasn't done. You weren't around then to know, to see—"

"I didn't have to be around to know the truth." She turned to Ken. "Do you remember what happened with Peter and me? How I never told him the truth about our finances, and the disastrous results of that?"

Ken nodded, not seeing her point, as she continued.

"Do you remember how I felt when you went behind my back to Peter, trying to help me? And our talk afterward? We decided it was wrong to hold back from someone you love, wrong to do their thinking for them, even if it was for their own good." She took a deep breath and turned to look at each of the Radnor brothers in turn. "Well, that's what's happened here."

"I know what you're saying, but how does it relate to Carmichael and us?" Ken asked.

Janet turned to the back of her folder and held out an envelope. The same envelope that Douglas Carmichael had given to her the night of the party. Her insurance. With Ken's acceptance of the plan, she knew the battle was won, but she was sure Doug wouldn't resent it if she showed all three brothers the letter now.

"What is that, Janet?" Ken asked.

She handed him the envelope and watched as he opened it and read the short, scribbled note. His face registered shock, acceptance and perhaps a bit of remorse.

"Why didn't Doug ever show this to us before?"

"He gave his word to your father. It was important for him to keep that promise."

"What is it?" Brian asked. "What does it say?"

Ken sighed. "It's a letter from Dad."

Edmund jumped from his seat. "What? It can't be!"

"It is, Ed. I recognize the handwriting. I'll read it:

"Douglas,
It's almost over now. You've done well with the bid, exactly as I've said. As soon as the paperwork is processed on Bradford, we'll get the ball rolling on Plan B—to merge our two companies. The boys don't know, of course, but it's better this way—less trouble and all. Soon, my boy, we'll all be together. It's what I've always wanted, to be sure. We'll talk next week.

"It's signed 'Gil.'" Ken handed the note to Edmund. "It's dated two days before he died."

The three brothers looked at one another, painful memories surfacing, with a wave of understanding replacing the hostility they'd known for so long.

Edmund studied the paper, fingered it as if it were a living link to the father he'd loved and respected. "Why didn't he tell us?"

"I think he wanted it to look like a straight business deal," Janet said. "With no favoritism toward Doug on his part. He loved Doug as if he were one of his own and to your father, bringing Doug into the company would have completed the circle." She paused and looked at each of them. "He also wanted to save face with you. For so many years he was adamant about his 'family only' policy that he became trapped by his own edict." She leaned forward. "He wanted Doug on the board, but his pride kept him from admitting it. So, the merger with Bradford was his way of making it seem like a good business deal with no explanations needed."

Edmund stared at her for a moment, deep in thought; then he nodded at the wisdom of her words. "I suppose we owe Mr. Carmichael a rather large apology," he said softly. "All of us." He turned back to Janet. "And you, young lady, this was a very brave thing you did today. I must rethink my feelings about you, too." He took her hand and smiled.

Janet returned the smile and squeezed Edmund's hand in response. "I'd like that, Edmund."

Brian came around the table and hugged her. "You're amazing! Why didn't you tell me about the note?"

"I didn't know about it until the other night. And I promised Doug I wouldn't use it unless absolutely necessary. Edmund's reaction qualified, don't you think?"

Brian laughed. "Yeah, I think you could correctly call that a necessity!" He turned to his brothers. "If you don't need me anymore, I've got to run."

"Go," Edmund said as he piled the folders one on top of the other.

Ken walked over to Janet. "You've won," he said with a mixture of emotions evident in his voice.

"We all did," she answered, and then, eyes shimmering, she whispered, "Thank you."

The door opened and the secretary poked her head in. "Excuse me," she said, "there's someone here to see you."

The door swung open to reveal Douglas Carmichael standing by the threshold.

"Doug!" Janet called, and almost ran to him. He opened his arms and hugged her.

"I hope you don't mind. I had to come. I couldn't wait for a phone call!"

"We did it!" She smiled broadly.

"I know. Brian just told me on his way out. You're one fantastic lady!" He hugged her again.

Ken watched their exchange uneasily, his feelings jumbled. He knew a lifelong rivalry could not automatically be converted to a friendship in a matter of minutes. And although his rational side now accepted and acknowledged Doug as friend rather than foe, he couldn't stop the tightening of his stomach muscles at the sight of his wife in the man's arms.

As he faced the smiling pair, an irrefutable fact hit him square between the eyes. Without the threat Douglas had presented, he and Janet would never have married. A smile creased his face. He supposed he *did* have a lot to thank Douglas Carmichael for, after all.

Ken stepped forward as Doug gently disengaged himself from Janet. The two men stood eye to eye for a long, silent moment. Ken extended his hand and Doug readily took hold of it.

"I'm sorry," Ken said. "For a lot of things over the years, but most of all, for this." He held up the note. "It might take me a long time to make this up to you, Doug, but I'd like to try if you'll let me."

Doug grinned from ear to ear. "Apology accepted. You have nothing to make up to me. Being in business together makes up for it all. I think Gil's looking down at us right now and smiling."

Ken shook his hand again. "I think so, too. But at least let me buy you a drink, or dinner, or something. I know we have a lot of talking to do."

"I have an idea," Janet interjected. "Why not invite Doug to the town house in the city and I'll cook dinner?"

"Can you cook?" Ken asked.

Janet shrugged. "We can always order out."

"Done!" Doug said with a slap on Ken's back and a laugh.

Edmund came forward and he and Doug also shook hands. "You and I have a great deal to talk about, Carmichael. How about coming into my office for a meeting now?"

Janet laughed out loud as Doug groaned. She guessed he'd heard of Edmund's infamous meetings.

"Okay, Ed," Doug said. "But let me warn you. I break for lunch!"

Janet and Ken watched the two men disappear down the hall. Ken turned her toward him.

"Can we go home now?" he asked. "I think we also need to talk."

"Yes," she said. "I think we do."

The ride back home was silent, each lost in thought. Janet was excited, on a natural high from the events of the morning, but she sensed Ken's mood wasn't as jubilant as her own. He seemed too quiet and closed, and she wondered why his private thoughts would trouble him so. He should be happy, as carefree as she. It was over. With this new merger, the Radnors would be able to buy her out, and the stock would no longer stand between her and Ken; Carmichael was no longer an enemy. They were free.

Janet would have been surprised to know that Ken's thoughts paralleled hers exactly. But his interpretation was slightly different. They were free all right, but to do what? What would she do now? Stay? Or go? She could afford Peter's schooling on her own, as well as a home of her own. There was nothing to keep her with him, except perhaps her love for him. God, he hoped it was as strong as his was for her.

They entered the house and went directly to their rooms. Ken fiddled with the keys while Janet removed her suit jacket and laid it across the chair. She turned to look at him. He looked nervous, wary. She walked over to him and took his hand.

Ken laughed nervously. "You know something? My head is flying right now! I've done something this morning that went against everything I believed. Then you pulled out that letter and I nearly died! My own father, the spy! How like him! I thought. It all made so much sense. He was always making decisions for us. Why didn't we see what he was doing with Doug? Why didn't we *know*?"

"Because you were blinded ... by ..."

"Jealousy. Go ahead, say it. It's true. We were all jealous of how Dad treated Doug. As if that somehow took his attention and love away from us. It's why I was such a bastard toward Doug when we were growing up. I know that now."

"Don't berate yourself, Ken. You couldn't have known what your father was doing. And under the circumstances, blaming Doug wasn't so farfetched."

He dropped her hand and ran his through his hair. "I know, I know. But it doesn't make it any easier. I feel like a heel. What must Carmichael think of us?"

"Doug came to terms with all of you years ago. He's content to let sleeping dogs lie. He has what he wants."

"And you?" he asked. "Do you have what you want, Janet?"

"I don't know, do I?"

"Well, you have your money. That's a start."

"True. I'm more at ease knowing Peter will be taken care of."

"So. What now? What about us?"

"Well, I guess we have to decide what we want. If we want to stay married and all." Her eyes beseeched him. "That is, if you want me."

Ken pulled her into his arms and buried his face in her hair. "Oh, sweetheart, through all this, that's the one thing I've always been sure of. Nothing else seems to matter as much as that . . . I don't know why."

She reached up and stroked his brow with her forefinger. "Don't you?" she asked. "I do." She stood on tiptoe and kissed his chin, his cheek, and lightly brushed her lips against his. "Because you love me," she whispered, "and because I love you."

He stared at her for a long, intense moment, and she lost herself in those dark, familiar eyes. Then his mouth was on hers, his tongue insinuating itself into the recesses of her mouth, mimicking the act of love. He reached up and untied the bow at the top of her blouse and opened the top button. Reaching inside with both hands, he unhooked her bra. He broke the kiss and looked down at her full breasts. He rubbed his thumbs across the nipples, now taut with arousal.

"I've missed you," he said.

Then he brought his lips to her breasts, working magic on her sensitive nipples. He flicked his tongue across the points, laving them. He nipped gently, sending shock waves all the way down to her toes. She arched her back until she could go no farther. And then she began pulling at the buttons of his shirt, pulling off his jacket. The need to touch him, to feel the heat of his naked flesh against her hands, was second only to the need to be filled by him totally and completely. The ache grew and she whimpered at its intensity.

The sound triggered an instant response in Ken. He pulled at the remainder of her suit and, one by one, items of clothing hit the floor to pool around her feet. He stopped for a moment in awe at the sight of her as she stood there clad only in her panties, pale blue and shimmering lace.

He took off his shirt, tie and jacket, his overbright eyes never leaving the vision before him.

"Oh, sweetheart," he said as he took her hand and placed it on him. "Feel me, feel what you do to me."

Janet moved her hand over him and felt his arousal through the material of his pants. She basked in the feeling of power it gave her to know she could create such a response in him so quickly with a look, a touch, a gesture. Reaching down, she slowly pulled on the zipper and slipped her hand into the opening, tentatively at first, then bolder, as she caressed him.

Ken groaned under the assault, his senses soaring as he insinuated his fingers under the elastic band of her panties to find that secret sacred place that was his and his alone. She was ripe and ready for him, and he delved deeper until she collapsed against him.

They fell to their knees, facing each other, in the living room in front of the coffee table, in the middle of the day, uncaring where they were. They were lost in another world inhabited only by lovers in the heat of passion.

Their bodies strained the confines of their remaining clothes. Janet released him from the restraining briefs and moved her hand over him. He was completely aroused and erotically smooth. Unable to bear her gentle touch any longer, Ken stretched the elastic band of her panties and thrust himself into her warm, welcoming body.

He rolled them backward onto the floor, and she found herself astride him, in absolute control. She took full advantage of it.

"That's it. Oh, honey, that's it." Ken smiled, delighted with her in every way.

She moved over him, rotating her hips, throwing back her head, uncaring of what remained of their clothes or anything else. Ken guided her movement with his hands as his thumbs gently met in the middle, caressing her gently, sending tiny sparks shooting through her system.

It was upon her before she could prepare for it. The spasm rocked her body and she called out his name, over and over again in a litany of love. He pulled her down to him and kissed her deeply, providing a buffer as the tremors subsided. They tumbled over, and he continued to move within her, her urgency giving way to his, as he, too, reached the peak of fulfillment.

He kissed her mouth again and again, holding her tightly to him, as if he would never, ever, let her go.

"Say it again," he demanded.

"I love you."

"Again."

"I love you."

He let out a long-held sigh and relaxed his grip. They separated, but didn't part. He ran a hand through her tangled hair adoringly.

"Will you marry me?" he asked.

Janet grinned. "Silly man. We *are* married. Very much married, I'd say."

Ken shook his head. "But I never *did* get to ask you. Edmund asked Paul Bradly. And when we said those vows, neither of us meant it." He stared into her fathomless eyes.

"I want to mean it," he whispered. "I want to do it again."

Tears filled her eyes and her throat constricted, the depth of her emotion almost too much to bear.

"So will you?" he prompted.

She nodded, unable to find her voice to speak.

Ken toyed with her hair, wrapping a golden strand around his fingers. "Let's go somewhere alone. Maybe upstate to that inn we stayed at when we visited Peter. Maybe he'll even come this time. What do you think?"

The tears spilled over onto her cheeks, running tracks down onto the rug. "I think I couldn't be more in love with you, or proud of you, if I tried."

"Proud?"

"Yes. Very. For what you did today. For taking my side at the meeting." She touched the shell of his ear with her fingertip. "Even *before* you knew about your father's letter."

"It's as you said. It was a good deal."

She shook her head. "No. It wasn't the deal. It was me. You came through for me."

He kissed her. "Yes," he said, "for you. Because I love you, Janet. I think I always have, from that very first day, that very first kiss."

"No one ever kissed me like that before. I'm afraid I didn't quite know what I was doing."

"Oh, no? Well, you certainly are a fast learner," he teased.

She smiled dreamily. "Only for you, always for you."

He kissed the tip of her nose. "Promise?"

She nodded. "I'll even put it in writing."

*   *   *   *   *

You'll flip . . . your pages won't!
Read paperbacks *hands-free* with

Book Mate · I

The perfect "mate" for all your romance paperbacks

**Traveling • Vacationing • At Work • In Bed • Studying
• Cooking • Eating**

Perfect size for all standard paperbacks, this wonderful invention makes reading a pure pleasure! Ingenious design holds paperback books OPEN and FLAT so even wind can't ruffle pages— leaves your hands free to do other things. Reinforced, wipe-clean vinyl-covered holder flexes to let you turn pages without undoing the strap . . . supports paperbacks so well, they have the strength of hardcovers!

Pages turn WITHOUT opening the strap.

SEE-THROUGH STRAP

Reinforced back stays flat.

Built in bookmark

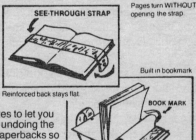

BOOK MARK

BACK COVER HOLDING STRIP

10˝ x 7¼˝, opened.
Snaps closed for easy carrying, too

Available now. Send your name, address, and zip code, along with a check or money order for just $5.95 + .75¢ for postage & handling (for a total of $6.70) payable to Reader Service to:

Reader Service
Bookmate Offer
901 Fuhrmann Blvd.
P.O. Box 1396
Buffalo, N.Y. 14269-1396

Offer not available in Canada
*New York and Iowa residents add appropriate sales tax.

BM-G